"You know you don't have to do this if you don't want to."

His sideways glance carried total exasperation. "If you think for one moment I'm going to let you back out now, then you have another think coming!"

"Yes, but if you don't really want to...."

"Don't *want* to?" he grated out. "I'm sitting here in agony, I want you so much. I've thought of nothing else all night!"

"Oh." Molly was stunned, then thrilled by the dark frustration in his voice.

"Look, just in case you're languishing under a misapprehension here," Liam went on irritably, "it's passion that sends men to bed with women, not compassion. I wanted you the moment I saw you."

MIRANDA LEE

The Seduction Project

Passion™

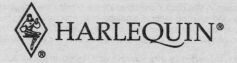

HARLEQUIN®

TORONTO • NEW YORK • LONDON
AMSTERDAM • PARIS • SYDNEY • HAMBURG
STOCKHOLM • ATHENS • TOKYO • MILAN • MADRID
PRAGUE • WARSAW • BUDAPEST • AUCKLAND

ISBN 0-373-12003-6

THE SEDUCTION PROJECT

First North American Publication 1999.

CHAPTER ONE

TWENTY-FIVE today, Molly thought as she brushed her hair back from her high forehead and coiled its straight brown length on top of her head.

A quarter of a century.

Sighing, Molly inserted the first of six securing pins without having to look at what she was doing. She'd done her hair like this for the last few years. It was easy and practical and, above all, cheap. She needed every spare cent from her pay packet to make ends meet.

At last she glanced up into the vanity mirror and surveyed the finished product with a wry smile. There was no doubt she looked the stereotyped concept of a librarian through and through. Prim hairdo. Prissy blouse. Pleated skirt. All she needed was horn-rimmed glasses balancing on the end of her none too small nose to complete the staid image.

Molly had twenty-twenty vision, however. Which was unfortunate in some respects. How much kinder it would be, she imagined, to have a fuzzier reflection first thing every morning.

She suddenly saw herself looking in the bathroom mirror on her fiftieth birthday and nothing would have changed much, not even her hairstyle.

She would still be living at home with her mother.

She would still be plain.

And she would still be madly in love with Liam.

Her shudder was part despair, part self-disgust. For loving Liam was such a waste of time; such a waste of her life.

Molly knew he would *never* love her back.

She no longer clung to the teenage fantasy where Liam woke up one day and saw that his feelings for the girl next door had somehow miraculously changed overnight from platonic friendship to an all-consuming passion. By the time she turned twenty-one, Molly had graduated from romantic to realist. Difficult to hold onto such a futile dream in the face of the type of girl Liam brought home with regular monotony.

'Plain' did not describe them. Neither did blue-stocking, nor bookworm, as Molly had been labelled all her life. Liam's girlfriends were better known for their bodies than their brains. He liked them tall and tanned, with long legs, lush breasts and hair which shimmered.

Molly told herself she had the right breasts, but nothing short of the rack was going to add four inches to her average height. And, while her hair was always clean and healthy, mousy brown just never seemed to shimmer.

So Molly had long since abandoned any romantic schoolgirl dreams when it came to Liam. Common sense told her he was a lost cause. Yet still she clung to the emotion of loving him, clung to it as a drowning man clung to the most tenuous lifeline. Why else was she living in this house which was far too big for just two people, and far too expensive?

Because Liam's family lived next door, that was why. If Molly and her mother moved, she would never see him again. Never feel the joy—as bittersweet as it was—of having him drop in for a drink and a chat, as he did every once in a while.

Liam called her his best friend, but Molly knew she wasn't really that. She was simply *there*, a convenience, a ready ear to listen and give him feedback on his latest computer game or graphic design idea.

A deep dismay momentarily filled her soul before it was abruptly banished by a surprising burst of anger. How could Liam be so blind? And so darned insensitive? And why did *she* have to go on wallowing in his lukewarm and highly one-sided version of their being 'best friends'?

Best friends were supposed to share things, weren't they? Where was the give and take in their relationship? Today was her birthday, damn it. But would he remember? Not on your nelly! The dynamic head of Ideas and Effects Pty Ltd couldn't be expected to remember such trivia. He was far too busy running his excitingly successful business. Heck, he hardly had time to come home any more! She hadn't sighted him since Christmas, a full two months back.

There would be no phone call. No card, let alone a present. Yet she'd shopped for hours to find him the right gift for *his* birthday last year. She'd even cooked him a cake!

'Molly,' her mother called out through the bathroom door. 'What's taking you so long in there? Your breakfast's been on the table for a full five minutes.'

'Coming!'

Breakfast that morning was a small glass of orange juice, one boiled egg, one thin slice of wholemeal toast, one teaspoon of margarine and black coffee. A big improvement on the minute bowl of cereal Molly usually ate.

Ever since her father had died of a heart attack two years before at the relatively young age of fifty-one, her mother had become obsessed with health and dietary matters. Nothing passed their lips these days that exceeded the strict fat and calorie limits which were now Ruth McCrae's culinary bible.

This meant mealtimes held little joy for Molly, who had a chronically sweet tooth. She found it all a bit trying, yet could not deny that her once plump curves had benefited from this change of eating habits. She'd dropped two dress sizes and would now not shrink from going to the beach—if she hadn't freckled like mad.

'Wow!' she exclaimed as she sat down at the kitchen table. 'This looks really good.'

'Well, it *is* your birthday, love,' Ruth said. 'I'm going to cook you a special dinner tonight as well.'

Molly could not help wondering what a 'special' dinner constituted these days. She'd bet it wasn't baked pork with crackling and crispy roast potatoes, followed by a big chocolate cake and coffee with cream in it. 'That'll be nice, Mum,' she said, and picked up her knife, ready to attack the boiled egg.

'Aren't you going to open your card?' Ruth asked plaintively.

Molly could have kicked herself. She put down her knife and picked up the long white envelope propped against the fruit bowl. Inside was a sweetly sentimental card and a couple of lottery tickets which promised first prize of half a million dollars.

'I'm sorry I couldn't afford more,' her mother said apologetically.

Molly glanced up with a bright smile. 'Don't be silly. This is great. I might win a fortune and then we could both go for a trip around the world.'

'Oh, I wouldn't want to do that. I like my home too much. But you could go, I suppose,' she added hesitantly.

Molly could see that this idea did not sit well with her mother. Perhaps she was already regretting giving her daughter the chance—however slim—of becoming rich and possibly flying the nest.

Ruth McCrae was a naturally shy woman, who'd become even more reserved and reclusive since her husband's death. She rarely left the house except to go shopping, and that was only down to the small local shopping centre which also housed the library branch where Molly worked. She had no close friends and lived for her house, her garden and her daughter.

Once in a while, Molly found her mother's dependence on her stifling. But on the whole she accepted her fate without undue distress. She was, after all, her mother's daughter, which meant she was a quiet, undemanding girl with few unsettling yearnings.

The only yearning which could disturb her dreams—as well as her equilibrium—was Liam. Even then, she'd learned to control her unrequited passion for him. Clearly, he'd never guessed what smouldered behind her cool green eyes whenever they looked upon his handsome face.

And he never would.

This realisation suddenly brought another stab of anger. But this time none of it was directed at Liam. All of it was channelled straight at herself.

You're a fool, Molly! If it was one of your girlfriends pining after some man who was way out of their reach, you'd tell her to forget him and move on. It's about time you took your own advice.

Forget Liam. Move on!

Molly picked her knife up again and sliced the top off her egg with one decisive stroke. That was going to be her from now on. Decisive.

And her first decision was to stop fantasising about Liam and move on!

CHAPTER TWO

MOLLY was standing at the library computer, running the wand over the first of the huge pile of returned books, when something caught her eye. Something bright and red.

She glanced up through the glass doors to see a shiny red car turning its brand-new nose into the empty parking space right outside the library.

It brought no flash of recognition, despite being a very memorable model. Not quite a sports car, it was still stylish and expensive-looking. A newcomer to the area, no doubt, not knowing that this particular library branch was closed to the public on a Wednesday morning.

Molly was about to return to the job at hand when the driver's door opened and a heart-joltingly familiar head of hair came into view, gleaming golden under the summer sun.

Liam.

Her heart leapt. So he *had* remembered her birthday. He'd even come in person. She could hardly believe it!

Her happiness knew no bounds as she watched him close the car door and stride up onto the pavement

11

and across to the front doors. He smiled at her through the glass as he tap-tapped on the wooden frame.

'Can't they see we're closed?' Joan complained from where she was sitting at her desk, flipping through one of the new publisher catalogues. She could not see who was knocking. If she had, she would not be so anxious to send the unwanted visitor away. Joan might be a happily married thirty-three-year-old woman with three children, but she still had an eye for a good-looking man.

Liam was just that—and more. At thirty, he was in his physical prime, his elegant body in perfect tune with his equally elegant face. Six feet two inches tall, his lean frame made him look even taller, as did his choice of clothing. He had this thing for jackets, wearing them all year round.

In winter they ranged from soft suede numbers to tweedy sports coats. In summer he chose linen or lightweight wool in neutral colours, and teamed them with cool T-shirts during the day and silk shirts at night. Ties rarely graced his neck. In fact, Molly had never seen Liam dressed formally.

Today he was wearing stonewashed blue jeans, a navy T-shirt and a loose cream linen jacket with sleeves pushed up to the elbows. His streaky blond hair was longer than when she'd seen him last, falling to his ears from its side parting and flopping with its usual rakish charm across his high forehead. He looked slightly wind-blown and utterly gorgeous.

Molly immediately put her 'moving on' decision

on hold for a good five years. Thirty, she decided anew, was soon enough to give up all hope.

The fact that Liam was standing where he was at this very moment *had* to give her some hope. Fancy him abandoning his precious business on a working day to drive the fifty miles from Sydney to Gosford, just to see her on her birthday.

'For pity's sake!' Joan snapped when Liam knocked a second time. 'Can't they read? The library times are on the darned door!'

'It's someone I know,' Molly said. 'I'll just go let him in.'

Joan jumped up from her desk. 'But it's almost...' The sight of Liam's handsome self stopped her in her tracks. 'Mmm. Yes, by all means let him in,' she murmured, primping her glossy black waves as Molly hurried out from behind the reception desk and across the functional grey carpet.

Molly wasn't worried that Liam would find Joan attractive. As pretty as she was, she was a married woman.

Liam believed in keeping his sex life simple.

'One girl at a time,' he'd once confided in Molly. 'And never anyone else's.'

It was a surprisingly conservative attitude in this day and age, especially coming from a man who looked like Liam, who had women throwing themselves at him all the time.

He had a similarly strict attitude to marriage. Only one per lifetime, which was why he'd always said he would not bother with marriage till he was in his thirties and financially secure. He didn't want to make a mistake in finding his perfect partner.

'In the meantime,' he'd joked to her one day, 'I'm having a lot of fun auditioning possible future candidates for the position of Mrs Liam Delaney.'

It had always terrified Molly that one of those future candidates might capture Liam's love as well as his lust. Fortunately, that hadn't happened, and Molly had taken heart from the failure of his various very beautiful girlfriends to last more than a few months.

But his latest was a bit of a worry. A statuesque blonde who went by the name of Roxy, she'd already lasted six months—a record for Liam. He'd even brought her home with him for the Christmas break, during which time Molly had had many opportunities to see Roxy's physical assets. What she could do for a bikini was incomparable!

But I'm not going to think about Roxy right now, Molly told herself as she turned the key and swept open the door. Today is my birthday and my very best friend has come to celebrate it with me.

'Liam!' she exclaimed, smiling up into his dancing blue eyes.

'Hi there, Moll. Sorry to interrupt. I know you're working but I simply had to show you my new car. Picked it up this morning at one of those dealerships just the other side of Hornsby and couldn't resist taking it for a spin. Before I knew it I was on the expressway and heading north. I was over the

Hawkesbury Bridge before you could say boo, and was about to turn round when I thought, What the hell, Liam? You haven't had a day off in ages. Drive up to Gosford and visit your mum.'

He smiled a rueful smile, showing perfect teeth and a charming dimple. 'It wasn't till I pulled into the driveway that I remembered today is her golf day. Took all the wind out of my sails, I can tell you. But no way was I going back to Sydney without showing someone. Naturally, I thought of you. So what do you think of it?' And he waved in the direction of the car. 'It's one of the new Mazda Eunos 800s. The Miller Cycle version. Great red, isn't it?' he finished.

Every drop of joy drained out of Molly. Liam hadn't come for her birthday. He'd come to show her a pathetic car. Worse, she hadn't even been his first choice of viewer. She'd run a very poor second. As usual!

Something hard curled around her heart, setting it in concrete and trapping her love for him deep inside. Molly determined it would never see the light of day again. She glanced coldly over at the offending car and shrugged dismissively.

'If you've seen one red car, Liam,' she said coolly, 'you've seen them all.'

There was no doubt he was taken aback by the icy indifference of her tone, for his eyebrows shot up and he stared at her with bewilderment in his beautiful blue eyes.

Molly was disgusted with herself for instantly feeling guilty. So much for her first foray into hating Liam! But she was determined not to weaken this time. Enough was enough.

'You know me, Liam,' she went on brusquely. 'I've never been a car person.'

'That's because you've never learned to drive, Moll. You'd appreciate cars much more if you were ever behind the wheel. Come on, come for a short spin with me.' He actually took her arm and began propelling her across the pavement.

'Liam!' she protested, wrenching her arm away from his hold and planting her sensible shoes firmly on the pavement. 'I *can't*. I'm at work.'

'But the library's not even open,' he argued. 'Surely they won't miss you for a couple of minutes?'

'That's beside the point,' she said sternly. 'You might be your own boss, Liam, and can come and go as you please, but most people can't, me included. Besides, it's almost morning tea and I have to be here for that.'

The rest of the staff had all chipped in to buy her a cake. It was a tradition in the library whenever one of them had a birthday. No way was she going to run out on her real friends to indulge Liam's ego.

'I don't see why,' he said stubbornly.

No, you wouldn't, Molly thought mutinously, and toyed with telling him, just so he could feel terrible for a full ten seconds.

The decision was taken out of her hands when Joan popped her head out the door.

'Come on, birthday girl. Greg's brought your cake along and all twenty-five candles are alight and waiting. So get in here and do the honours. You can bring your hunk of a friend, if you like,' she added, looking Liam up and down with saucily admiring eyes. 'We've more than enough cake for an extra mouth.'

Molly relished Liam's groan. To give him some credit he did look suitably apologetic once Joan disappeared.

'God, Moll, I had no idea it was your birthday. There I was, blathering away about my new car, and all that time you must have been thinking how damned selfish I was being.'

Frankly, she was enjoying his guilt. It had a deliciously soothing effect on her damaged pride. 'That's all right, Liam. I'm used to your not remembering my birthday.'

He winced anew. 'Don't make me feel any more rotten than I already do.'

Molly almost gave in. It was awfully hard to stay mad at Liam. He didn't *mean* to be selfish. He was, unfortunately, the product of a doting mother and far too many God-given talents. Brains *and* beauty did not make for a modest, self-effacing kind of guy. Liam could be generous and charming when he set his mind to it, but in the main he was a self-absorbed individual who rarely saw beyond the end of his own classically shaped nose.

God knows why I love him so much, Molly thought irritably.

But then her eyes travelled slowly from his perfect face down over his perfect body, and every female cell she owned clamoured to be noticed back.

But the only expression in *his* eyes when he looked down at her was remorse. When he forcibly linked arms with her, she glared her frustration up to him.

'Don't be mad at me, Moll,' he said with disarming softness.

'I'm not mad at you,' she returned stiffly.

'Oh, yes, you are. And you have every right to be. But I'll make it up to you tonight, if you'll let me.'

'Tonight?' she echoed far too weakly.

'Yes, tonight,' he said firmly. 'But for now I think your colleagues are waiting for you to blow out those twenty-five candles.'

With typical Liam confidence he steered her into the library and proceeded to charm everyone in the place. It annoyed Molly that he gave her openly curious workmates the impression he was a boyfriend of sorts. He even extracted her promise in Joan's goggle-eyed presence to go out with him later that evening. She initially refused dinner—no way was she going to disappoint her mother—but grudgingly agreed to after-dinner coffee somewhere.

Molly told herself afterwards that she would *never* have agreed to go out with him at all if she'd been alone with him. She would have sent him on his way with a flea in his ear! She didn't need his pity, or his guilt.

The moment his new red Mazda roared off up the

road back in the direction of Sydney, Joan settled drily knowing eyes on her.

'Well, you're a dark horse, Molly, aren't you?' she said as they walked together back into the library. 'I've always thought of you as a quiet little thing and all this time you had something like *that* on the side.'

Molly silently cursed Liam to hell. All he ever caused her was trouble and heartache. 'Liam's mother lives next door,' she explained with more calm than she was feeling. 'I've known Liam for years. We're just good friends.'

'Oh, *sure*. He drove all the way up from Sydney to wish you a happy birthday because you're just *good friends*. You know what? I'll bet you're one of those girls who go home from the office at night, and perform one of those ten-second transformations. You know the type. Off come the glasses and the strait-laced clothes. Down comes the hair. On goes the sexy gear, make-up and perfume, and—whammo!—instant heat!'

Molly had to laugh. It would take more than ten seconds to transform *her*!

'You can laugh,' Joan scoffed. 'But I'm no one's fool. And you're far prettier than you pretend to be. I always did wonder why you never seemed to be on the lookout for a fella. I was beginning to think all sorts of things till glamour boy arrived on the scene today. He gave *me* a case of instant heat, I can tell you. And I saw the way *you* looked at him when you didn't think anyone was noticing. You've got it bad,

Molly. I know the signs. So why haven't I heard of this paragon of perfection before? Why all the mystery and secrecy? Is he married? A womaniser? A bad boy? Look, you can trust me with your deep dark secrets,' she whispered. 'I won't tell anyone.'

Molly laughed a second time. 'There's nothing deep *or* dark to tell. I repeat…we're just good friends. As I said before, Liam used to live next door. We went to school together, though not in the same class. He was doing his HSC when I was only in my first year.'

'Well, there's nothing remotely boy-next-door about him any more,' came Joan's dry remark. 'He has city written all over him. Not to mention success.'

'I'm well aware of that, believe me. I'm not blind. But there's never been any romance between us, and there never will be. He has a steady girlfriend. Goes by the name of Roxy.'

'Roxy,' Joan repeated, her nose wrinkling. 'Don't tell me. She's a stunning blonde with boobs to die for, hair down to her waist and legs up to her armpits.'

Molly was startled. 'You know her?'

'Nope. Just guessed. Men like your Liam always seem to have girls like that on their arm.'

'He isn't my Liam,' Molly said tightly.

'But you'd like him to be, wouldn't you?'

Molly opened her mouth to deny it. But her tongue failed her when a thickness claimed it. Tears pricked at the back of her eyes.

Her Liam.

What a concept. What an improbable, impossible, inconceivable, unachievable concept! To keep clinging to it was not only demeaning to her personally, but depressing in the extreme.

'There was a time when I did,' she said at last, her tone clipped and cold. 'But not any more. I have better things to do with my life than pine for the impossible.'

'Impossible? Why do you say it's impossible?'

'For pity's sake, Joan, you've seen him. You yourself said men like Liam go for girls like Roxy, not mousy little things like me.'

'You'd be far from mousy if you made the best of yourself. To be frank, Molly, a little make-up wouldn't go astray. And an occasional visit to the hairdresser.'

Molly stiffened, despite the criticism striking home. 'I wouldn't want a man who didn't love me for myself,' she said sharply.

'That's rubbish and you know it! I'm an old married lady and I still have to work hard to keep my man. Now you listen to me, Molly. When Liam comes to take you out tonight, surprise him.'

'Surprise him?'

'Yes. Leave your hair down. Slap some make-up on. Use a sexy perfume. Wear something which shows off that great little figure of yours.'

For a split second, Molly was buoyed up by Joan's compliment on her figure. But then she thought of

Roxy's tall, voluptuous, sex-bomb body...and her momentary high was totally deflated.

'I don't have any sexy perfume,' she muttered dispiritedly. She didn't own much make-up either. But she wasn't about to admit that.

Joan gave her an exasperated glare. 'Then buy some at the chemist during your lunch-hour!'

Their library was in a small regional centre which boasted quite a few shops, a well-stocked chemist shop included.

Molly declined telling Joan that she only had five dollars in her purse. Sexy perfume was expensive, and she'd rather wear nothing than douse herself in a cheap scent.

Molly was actually contemplating asking Joan to lend her some money when reality returned with a rush. She could wear more make-up than a Japanese geisha and drown herself in the most exotic expensive perfume in the world and it would not make Liam fall in love with her. To think otherwise was ludicrous in the extreme, and belittling to his intelligence.

'Thank you for your advice, Joan,' she said with a return to common sense, 'but I'd really rather just be myself. Now I'd better get back to these books.'

Molly resumed checking in the returns, blocking her mind to everything but the thought that at least she would not have to starve to death tonight after her mother's special birthday meal. Liam could buy her something delicious and creamy to go with her after-dinner coffee.

She gave no more thought to Joan's advice about make-up and perfume, till she arrived home late that afternoon and opened her carryall to find a paper parcel sitting on top of her house keys.

It contained a small but expensive-looking spray bottle of perfume.

And a note.

'Happy birthday, darls!' Joan had written in her usual extravagant hand. 'This always works for me. Well…sometimes. Still, what have you got to lose? Go for it!'

Molly sprayed a tiny burst of perfume onto her wrist and lifted it to her nose. It was a wonderfully sensual smell, its heavy musk perfume bringing images of satin sheets and naked bodies and untold unknown delights.

Molly shook her head. To wear such a scent in Liam's presence would be the ultimate self-torture.

And let's face it, Molly, she told herself, wearing perfume—no matter how sensual—isn't about to turn Liam into some kind of sex-crazed lunatic. With a girl like Roxy in tow, no doubt he has all the sex he can handle.

Molly glanced at the perfume's name and almost laughed. Seductress, it was called. Good Lord. It would have to be a powerful potion to turn her into that!

It was a nice thought of Joan's, but a total waste of time and money.

So was her advice. For Molly believed she *did* have

something to lose. Her self-respect. And possibly Liam's friendship. She would not risk her relationship with him—such as it was—by acting differently or provocatively. He was an intelligent man and would surely notice if she climbed into his car wearing such an overpoweringly sexy scent.

No. She would not do it. Neither would she change her hairstyle, or put on more make-up, or scrounge through her limited wardrobe in some vain attempt to find something more figure-revealing.

Molly had her pride.

She shoved the perfume back in her bag and extracted her house key.

'Is that you, dear?' her mother called out as she pushed open the front door.

'Yes, Mum.'

The smell of a roast dinner teased Molly's nostrils as she made her way along the hall and into the kitchen. Not a pork smell. Chicken.

Naturally, came the rueful thought. Chicken carried the least fat and calorie count, provided the skin was removed. Which it would certainly be. She almost sighed when she also spied her mother wrapping the hoped-for crispy baked potatoes in foil.

Ruth glanced up and smiled at her daughter. 'Have a good day, dear?'

'Pretty good. Joan and the others bought me a birthday cake for morning tea.'

'I hope you only had a small slice,' her mother said, frowning. 'I was going to get you a cake tonight but

I thought it an extravagance when we can't eat all of it.'

Molly suddenly felt like screaming. She turned away to hook her navy carryall over a chair, schooling her face into a more pleasant expression before turning back. 'You'll never guess who dropped in to see me this morning,' she said brightly.

'I can't think. Who?'

'Liam.'

'Liam? You mean Liam Delaney?'

'The one and the same.' Molly declined telling her mother about the fiasco of his new car. 'He was up this way today and asked me out tonight for my birthday.'

'But I'm cooking you a special dinner tonight!'

'I'll be here for dinner, Mum. Liam isn't picking me up till around eight.'

Ruth gave her daughter a sharp look. 'You do realise he already has a girlfriend? A very beautiful one too, if I recall rightly.'

Molly controlled her growing irritation with difficulty. 'I'm well aware of that, Mum, but we're only going somewhere for coffee. Don't forget Liam and I were friends long before Roxy came along.'

Ruth began to frown. 'I still don't know about this. I have an awful feeling it's not a good idea.'

Molly came forward to give her mother a hug. 'Mum, stop worrying. I'm a big girl now and quite capable of looking after myself. Besides, it's not as though Liam is engaged or anything.'

Ruth's head jerked back and she looked at her daughter with worried eyes. 'You...you're not going to do anything you shouldn't do, Molly, are you?'

Molly was quite startled, and more than a little annoyed. 'Such as what?' It wasn't as though she was about to leap into bed with the man. Not that she wouldn't, if she ever had the chance. Making love with Liam was at the top of the list where her secret sexual fantasies were concerned. She was pretty sure, however, that she wasn't even *on* Liam's list.

'I...I don't know exactly,' her mother murmured. 'You seem different tonight...'

Molly now thanked her lucky stars that she wasn't attempting any kind of pathetic make-over tonight. She could just imagine what her mother would have said if she'd waltzed downstairs all dolled up and doused in Seductress.

'Liam and I are just good friends, Mum,' she repeated for what felt like the umpteenth time that day.

Molly was shocked when her mother looked at her the same way Joan had. 'Come now, Molly,' she said. 'I'm your mother. I know exactly how you feel about that man.'

'Yes...well, he doesn't feel the same way about me, does he?' came her taut reply.

'No. And neither will he. *Ever*.'

Molly could not believe the pain her mother's words brought her. It was one thing to tell herself there was no hope. Quite another to hear the futility

of her dreams spoken aloud and with such crushing finality.

'I realise that,' she countered, her throat thick with hurt. 'You don't have to tell me.'

Molly just managed to sweep from the room before she burst into tears.

CHAPTER THREE

AT FIVE to eight, Molly was standing at her bedroom window, watching for Liam's car. She doubted he would be late. Surprisingly, punctuality was now one of his virtues.

He hadn't always been like that. When Molly had first met Liam, and he'd been a computer-mad adolescent of seventeen, she could not count the number of times he'd been late for things. Back then, he'd always been working on some computer-based project, becoming totally absorbed as soon as he sat down in front of the screen. Time had had little meaning for him once his concentration was focused on his latest game, or graphic design.

Every morning, Molly would wait anxiously outside his house for him to accompany her to school—a job he'd volunteered for when some bullies had started hassling her on the walk to school. Barely minutes before the school bell was due to ring, Liam would come dashing out, yelling for her to start running.

How she kept up with his long legs she would never know. But hero-worship made you do things your body was incapable of, although in that final year she was to share school with Liam she hadn't yet reached puberty—or her fat phase—being only twelve. Somehow, she'd managed to stick to his shadow like glue all the way, down the hill then along the flat beside the railway, over the railway bridge, across the highway then up another hill to school, usually arriving in time but in a totally breathless state.

She would have to run home too, so that Liam could be sitting back down to his all-consuming hobby all the quicker. Although never interested in sport, Liam had been very fit in those days from running to and from school at full pelt. He still ran every day, jogging to and from work, apparently. He'd told her once that his best inspirations and ideas came while he was running.

Molly was about to turn away from the window when Liam's bright red car came up the hill and turned into their driveway. Right on time! She shook her head in rueful acceptance that Liam had changed in many ways. He was no longer the forgetful boy next door. He was an exceptionally sharp businessman. Ambitious. Brilliant. Successful.

Way out of your league, Molly.

Sighing, she bent to switch off her bedside lamp, and was about to leave the room when she hesitated, walking back to where she could watch Liam, unobserved, from the now darkened window.

He sat there for several seconds, combing his hair. Though not with undue vanity. He didn't even glance into the rear-vision or side-mirror, just swept the comb quickly through both sides and down the back before slipping it back into his jacket pocket.

At least in that Liam hadn't changed. He'd never been vain about his looks, and still wasn't. There was nothing of the peacock in him.

Yet, for all that, he did like to look good. Molly believed his sense of style came from his mother, who, though in her late fifties, was very young at heart and kept up to date with the latest trends and fashions. A writer and illustrator of children's books, Babs Delaney had ably supported herself and her only son after her husband was killed in a rock-climbing accident when Liam was only twelve.

It suddenly occurred to Molly how similar her and Liam's family backgrounds were. Both only children with widowed mothers.

But there the similarity ended. Babs Delaney was nothing like her own, timid mother. She was an outgoing personality with a wide range of friends and interests. She loved Liam to death but did not live her life through her son. She was encouraging, never clinging, a positive force, without a pessimistic or negative thought. She always said she wanted the best for her son, but that it was up to him to find what was best for himself.

It was no wonder Liam thought the world was his oyster; no wonder his business had been a great success. He'd even won an award a couple of years back as New South Wales Young Businessman of the Year and was often asked to be a motivating after-dinner speaker at various functions.

A quiver rippled down Molly's spine as she watched the object of her secret obsession unfold his elegant frame from behind the wheel. He was dressed in the same blue jeans, navy top and cream linen jacket he'd been wearing earlier. He stretched as he stood up, and another *deeper* quiver reverberated all through her.

For the first time it struck Molly just how intensely sexual her love for Liam had become with the passing of the years. Her more innocent schoolgirl crush had long since graduated to a full-on physical passion, filled with needs and yearnings which would not be denied. More and more she dreamt of making love with Liam, rather than just loving him. She would lie in bed at night and think about what it would be like to kiss him and touch him; how he would look, naked and erect; how he would *feel*, deep inside her.

She blushed in the darkness, her blood pounding through her body, her head whirling with a wild mixture of shame and excitement. Was she wicked to think about such things?

She didn't feel wicked. She felt driven and compelled, oblivious to everything but wanting Liam with a want that had no conscience, only the most merciless and agonising frustration. Oh, how she wished she were dazzlingly beautiful, with the sort of body no man could resist!

A bitter longing flooded Molly as she watched

Liam stride confidently towards her front door, his golden head gleaming under the street lights. Her grip on the curtains tightened and inevitably her thoughts turned to the dreaded Roxy.

How often did Liam sleep with her? she wondered enviously. Molly knew he didn't live with her, but that didn't mean they didn't share most of their nights either at his place or hers. Was she great in bed? came the added tormenting thought. Did she know all the tricks that a man would find irresistible? What was it she did to him that had kept Liam interested for six whole months?

Another awful possibility snuck into Molly's mind, twisting her heart and her stomach. Surely he couldn't *love* Roxy. Surely he wasn't going to *marry* her? Surely not.

The front doorbell rang, the sound jarring Molly's suddenly stretched nerves. She resisted rushing downstairs, her thoughts still simmering with resentment at the situation. She should not have agreed to go out with Liam tonight, not even for coffee. She was only torturing herself.

She heard her mother slide the door back from the family room then walk with small steps along the plastic strip which protected the hallway carpet. The front door creaked slightly on opening.

'Hello, Liam,' Ruth said with stiff politeness.

'Hello, Mrs McCrae. You're looking well.'

Molly listened to their small chat for a minute or two before gathering herself and coming downstairs, glad now that she hadn't made a superhuman effort with her appearance. Even so, her mother looked her up and down as though searching for some hint of secret decadence.

Molly doubted if even the most devious mind could find anything to criticise in her knee-length black skirt and simple white knitted top, even if the latter did have a lacy design and pretty pearl buttons down the front. Her choice of jewellery could hardly give rise to speculation, either. The string of pearls her own parents had given her for her twenty-first birthday was conservative and sedate, as were the matching pearl earrings.

The rest of her was equally sedate. Skin-coloured pantyhose, medium height black pumps, hair up in its usual knot and no make-up on except coral lipstick. Even her underwear was sedate. But only Superman with his X-ray vision could see that. Not that the sight of her modest white crossover bra and cotton briefs would send any man's heart aflutter.

Molly was at a loss to understand, then, why Liam himself frowned up at her as she came down the stairs. She had no illusions that he was struck by some previously untapped appreciation of her beauty. So why was he giving her the once-over with that slightly surprised look in his eyes?

Her curiosity was not satisfied till they were alone and walking along the curving front path towards his parked car.

'You know, Moll,' he said, 'you've lost quite a bit of weight lately, haven't you?'

Molly clenched her teeth down hard in her jaw. She'd been losing weight steadily for two years, and had been this size for at least three months. Hadn't he even noticed before this moment? What about at Christmas, or earlier today, at the library?

No, of course not. For the last six months his eyes had all been for Roxy. And this morning he'd been all wrapped up in his stupid new car.

'Not lately I haven't,' she replied coolly. 'I've been this weight for quite a while.'

'Oh? I didn't notice.'

Tell me something new, Molly thought tartly. She felt piqued that there wasn't the smallest change in him that *she* didn't notice. She knew whenever he'd had his hair cut; when he'd bought a new jacket; when he'd changed women.

'Are you sure Roxy won't mind your taking me out tonight?' she was driven to ask, barely controlling the lemony flavour in her voice.

'Roxy and I are having a trial separation,' he bit out.

'Oh?' Molly battled to look perfectly normal. Difficult when your stomach had just done a back-flip. 'You have a fight or something?'

'Or something,' he muttered.

'You don't want to tell me about it?'

His smile was wry as he wrenched open the passenger door. 'Not tonight, Moll. I don't want to spoil my mood by thinking about women.'

'But *I'm* a woman, Liam!' she pointed out archly.

'Yeah, but you're different. I don't really think of you like that. You're my friend. Come on. Get in. I'm going to drive us out to Terrigal. It's a lovely night for a walk along the beach.'

Which it was. Clear and warm, with stars sparkling in the night sky. A night for lovers.

Molly tried not to think about that. Masochism was not one of her vices.

Or maybe it was?

'But I'm not dressed for the beach,' she protested when Liam climbed in behind the wheel. 'I have high heels and stockings on for one thing.'

'You can take them off in the car,' he suggested without turning a hair.

His indifference to her undressing in front of him was depressing in the extreme. She could just imagine what would happen if Roxy started stripping in the passenger seat, wriggling her pouty bottom while she unpeeled her stockings down those long, tanned legs of hers. Liam wouldn't concentrate on his driving for long. Molly had an awful feeling that *she* could sit there stark naked in front of Liam and all he would do was ask her if she was cold!

Molly was saved from terminal depression by the lovely thought that dear Roxy seemed close to receiving her walking papers. Molly had hated her more than all of Liam's other women. Perhaps because she was the most beautiful. And the most confident in her position as Liam's girlfriend.

Molly's mood lightened considerably just thinking about Roxy's failure to be promoted to fiancée.

'I hope you don't think you're going to worm your way out of buying me coffee!' she told him while he reversed out of the driveway. 'I was going to order a big rich slice of cake with it. You've no idea, Liam, what food Mum has been feeding me ever since Dad died. She's become a ''fat-free for ever'' nutcase!'

'No worse than having a mother who wants to feed you up,' he countered drily. 'Every time I come home, Mum says I'm getting too thin, then out come the chips and the pastries and God knows what else.'

'You're not too thin,' Molly said. 'You're just right.'

He smiled over at her and her heart lurched. God, but he was heart-stoppingly handsome when he smiled.

'You know, you're good for me, Moll. You always say the right thing. And you always *do* the right thing,' he added meaningfully. 'You put me to shame today. I never remember your birthday and you always remember mine. So if you open the glove box in front of you there's a little something there which I hope will make up for all those other forgotten occasions.

'And don't tell me I shouldn't have,' he went on before she could open her mouth. 'And don't tell me it's too expensive. I can afford it. Fact is, I can afford pretty well whatever I want these days. That computer game I told you about some time back has just gone on the worldwide market and it's going to make me a multimillionaire.'

'Oh, Liam, that's wonderful!'

'Maybe,' he said drily. 'I'm beginning to find out being rich and successful isn't all it's cracked up to be. Except when it comes to buying my best friend something really nice,' he added with a warm smile. 'Go on. Rip the paper off and open it up. I'm dying to see what you think of it.'

Molly did just that, and gasped. 'Oh, Liam! You shouldn't have.'

'I thought I told you not to say that,' he said ruefully. 'Now, are you sure you like it? There were so many designs to choose from. I was in the jewellery shop for hours this afternoon trying to decide. In the end I settled for something simple, but solid. Like you.'

Molly tried to take his words as a compliment, but somehow some of the pleasure of his gift dissolved at that point. She lifted the heavy gold chain necklace from its green velvet bed, laying it across one palm while she slowly traced the heavy oval links with the index finger of her right hand.

Simple, but solid. Like me.

'You don't like it.'

Molly heard the disappointment in his voice and forced herself to throw him a bright smile. 'Don't be silly. I love it.' When his attention returned to the oncoming traffic, her eyes continued to secretly caress him for several moments. How could I not love it? was the heart-catching reality. It's from you, my darling. I will treasure it for the rest of my life.

Liam was frowning. 'I hope you're not just saying that.'

Molly found everything about the situation rather ironic. What would happen if she told him how she really felt about him? Knowing Liam, he would be terribly embarrassed. He hated complications in his life. He was a simple man at heart.

'Would I lie to you?' she quipped, though unable to keep the sardonic edge out of her voice.

He slanted her a rather bewildered look as though he'd never associated her with sarcasm before.

'Hmm. I hope not. You were always a brutally honest kid. But right on the ball. Why else do you think I used to ask your opinion on things? Mum would just say everything I wanted to do was great. I needed someone who told me as it really was. Which you did. When I think of the time I might have wasted on some of those airy-fairy projects I came up with. You were always able to make me see what was worth working on, Moll; what would last.'

A pity you never asked my opinion on your lady-friends, Molly thought wryly. I could have told you all those females loved themselves too much to have much left over for anyone else. But then, it wasn't love you wanted from them, was it, Liam?

Still, old habits die hard. What's going to happen

when you want a girl to love you, and whom you can truly love in return? You'll never find the right wife, gravitating towards the wrong type of girl. The Roxys of this world are only out for what they can get. Whereas I...I would love you as no other woman could ever love you, my darling. Look at me, Liam. Can't you see the love I bear you? Can't you *feel* it?

'Anyway, Moll,' Liam went on, oblivious of Molly's thoughts and feelings. 'I hope that necklace goes some small way to making up for my thoughtlessness in the past. I know I'm a selfish bastard. But your friendship means a lot to me and I wouldn't want you to think I never give you a moment's thought, because I do.

'Trouble is...' He threw her a wry smile. 'It's usually only when I need your help. Or your advice. Or your opinion on a new car.'

She didn't know whether to laugh or cry at that point. Anger, however, came to the rescue. 'And is that all tonight is, Liam?' she snapped. 'A test drive? Are you taking me all the way out to Terrigal just so you can get my opinion on your new car?'

'God, no!' He looked and sounded appalled. 'No, that's not it at all! Far from it. The thing is, I realised today down at the library that I never ask you about you. It added to my guilt, I can tell you. All these years and all we ever talk about is me. So tonight I want to hear all about *you*, Moll.'

'Me?' she echoed weakly.

'Yes. *You*. I want to know what's going on in your

life these days. You could have knocked me over with
a feather when that woman said you were twenty-five.
It suddenly came to me that a girl as great as you
should have been married by twenty-five. I began to
wonder why you're not. I wanted to ask you then and
there but it was hardly appropriate. So I'm asking you
now, Moll. Why haven't you got a boyfriend?'

Molly was really stumped. What to say? What to
tell him?

She busied herself putting the gold chain tidily into
its case and slipping it into her purse, all the while
trying to find the right lie to tell.

I just haven't met the right man yet...

I'm waiting till Mum gets over Dad's death...

I'd like to marry but the man I love doesn't even
know I'm alive in that sense...

The awkward silence grew till finally Liam shot her
a shocked look. 'Good God, Moll, you're not, are
you?'

'Not what?'

'Not...gay?'

CHAPTER FOUR

MOLLY'S eyes rounded. And then she laughed. That was one excuse she'd never thought of.

'No, I'm not gay.'

'So what's the problem?'

'The problem...' She considered her answer at some length, then decided excuse three carried a perverse kind of truth. Yet Liam—dear, sweet, blind Liam—would never guess. 'The problem is...that I *am* in love with a man. But he just doesn't love me back. In fact, he doesn't know I'm even alive in a sexual sense.'

'Why not?' Liam demanded to know, apparently affronted by this mystery man's lack of passion for his best friend.

Molly almost felt soothed by Liam's chagrin on her behalf. 'I guess I'm not his type, physically speaking. I'm not pretty enough.'

'What rubbish! You're *very* pretty.'

'No, I'm not, Liam. But it's nice of you to say so.'

Molly was grateful that Liam dropped the subject of her beauty. He scowled all through Gosford, not opening his mouth till they were on the Entrance Road and approaching Erina.

'So who is this idiot?' he flung at her. 'Is he a local?'

'Yes, of course.'

'Do I know him?'

'I should hope so.'

'Did he go to our school?'

'Yes. But that's as much as I'm going to say.'

'Our school...' He frowned as he scoured his memory. 'I can't think who it could be. Still, there were over eight hundred kids in our school.' He shook his head in frustration. 'I've no idea. Look, just tell me who he is. Don't keep me in suspense!'

'Sorry, but I'm not telling you, or anyone else for that matter. I would find it embarrassing. Besides, it's quite pointless my telling you who he is. I've pretty well accepted he's not interested. Shortly, I aim to get on with my life, so you don't have to worry, Liam. I don't intend to suffer indefinitely.'

Liam mumbled and muttered all through Erina, swinging the car around the large roundabout and heading for Terrigal before he launched into another verbal attack against her mystery man. Molly found it amusing that he was railing against himself.

'So! Does this splendid advertisement for feminine taste have a girlfriend?'

'Actually, he's between women at the moment.'

'Had a lot of them, has he?'

'Oodles.'

'And you *love* this inveterate ladies' man?'

'He takes my breath away.'

Liam pulled a face. 'What is it about women that they always fall for the bad guys? He sounds positively awful!'

'I don't think he's at all awful. And he's been very successful, businesswise.'

Liam's top lip curled into a sneer. 'I suppose he's good-looking.'

'Drop-dead gorgeous,' she agreed.

'Handsome is as handsome does, you know,' he growled, then muttered some more under his breath all the way to Terrigal.

Molly sat next to him in a self-satisfied silence. She hadn't enjoyed herself so much in years. Perhaps she was playing with a double-edged sword, but if so it was worth the risk. She didn't think the penny would drop for Liam. Meanwhile, she was experiencing a heady exhilaration in toying with the truth in this manner.

They came round the sweeping hillside corner which brought Terrigal beach into view and Molly sighed her pleasure at the sight. It was a pretty place during the day, but even more so at night, especially when it was cloudless, and the moon sent ribbons of silver rippling across the dark waters.

Tonight, the moonlight was strong, and the waves extra gentle as they lapped up onto the golden curve of sand. Some people were still swimming in the peaceful water. Many couples were sitting on the warm sand, arms around each other, or strolling along the beach, hand in hand. As Molly had thought earlier, it was a night for lovers.

Liam drove past the public car park at the bottom of the hill and along the narrow main street which flanked the beach, tall pines on the sea side, shops on the other. He eased into a space under a pine at the far end.

He snapped off his engine and swivelled in his seat to face Molly, a scowl on his handsome face. 'It's not Dennis Taylor, is it?'

Dennis Taylor was the only boy in Liam's class who could rival him for looks and subsequent business acumen. As dark as Liam was fair, he had thick black wavy hair, heavy-lidded dark eyes and the body of a bouncer. He did not have Liam's super intelligence or creative flair but he was a born salesman who'd gone into real estate after leaving school and done very well. He'd opened his own agency on the Central Coast a couple of years back and had recently expanded. Unmarried, he was a swinging bachelor type who played the field without mercy. He'd recently bought an acreage not far from Terrigal beach and built an orgy palace of a house, the rumoured activities therein supplying plenty of fuel for the local gossips.

Molly only knew Dennis as well as she did because his folks lived two doors up. He came to visit them quite often, and, Dennis being Dennis, he always waved at Molly if she was out the front watering or weeding the garden.

A couple of months back, he'd also knocked on the door and asked if she and her mother wanted to sell the house. Even after they'd said no, he'd left his business card then stayed talking to Molly for ages. He was one of those males who could not go past a female without proving he was God's gift to women. His charm operated on automatic pilot.

Molly found him likeable enough, but shallow. It irked her that Liam should think she could be madly in love with him.

'Well?' he probed. 'Is it?'

'I'm sorry but I refuse to answer any such questions on the grounds they might incriminate me.'

Liam glowered at her. 'You're being damned difficult.'

'I don't think so. You might be my friend but there's a limit to what I will tell you. And I think my love life is my own private business, don't you? After all, when I asked *you* what had happened between you and Roxy, you wouldn't tell me.'

'Hmm. Fair enough. But if it *is* Dennis,' he growled, 'then I hope to hell you never get your heart's desire. His reputation with women is appalling.'

Molly rolled her eyes. As if Dennis Taylor would take any serious notice of her anyway. That was as far-fetched as Liam doing so! Suddenly, she tired of this game. 'If it will make you feel any better,' she said wearily, 'then it's not Dennis. But please don't come up with any more candidates. I'm not going to tell you and that's that!'

'You've really dug your heels in about this, haven't you?'

'You could say that,' she pronounced, and crossed her arms with finality over her chest.

'I had no idea you could be this stubborn.'

Her sideways glance carried a sardonic flavour. 'There are quite a lot of things about me you don't know, Liam.'

'Mmm...I'm beginning to see that's the case. And there I've been all these years, telling people what a sweet little thing you are. It seems Roxy might not have been altogether wrong.'

Molly bristled. 'Oh? And what, pray tell, did dear Roxy say about me?'

'She said you were a sly piece and she wouldn't trust you as far as she could throw you.'

Molly's blood pressure rose a few notches. 'Humph! That's the pot calling the kettle black!'

'I take it you don't like Roxy?'

'You take it correctly.'

'Why?'

Molly almost launched into a tirade about vanity and superficiality and naked ambition, but pulled herself up just in time. There was little point in being vicious, now that the girl was possibly on the way out. Besides, the truth might sound too much like jealousy.

She managed a light shrug. 'You can't like every-

one in this world. Some people just rub you up the
wrong way right from the start.'

'True. Okay, I won't be a pain and press for more.
Neither will I ask you any more embarrassing questions about Mr X. I'm just relieved it's not Dennis.
Come on, let's go for that walk.' He was out of the
car before she could say Jack Robinson, bounding
around the front to her side where he wrenched open
the passenger door.

'Do…do you think we could have our coffee first?'
she asked a little shakily when Liam took her hand
and drew her upright out of the rather low-slung ve-
hicle. Whilst she told herself it was sheer hunger caus-
ing her stomach to cramp suddenly, she rather suspected there was another cause, and extracted her
hand from Liam's as soon as she could.

'I guess so,' he returned with a casual shrug. 'If
you're dying for some.'

'It's not the coffee I'm dying for so much as something to eat.'

Liam frowned. 'Haven't you had dinner? You told
me your mother was cooking dinner for you tonight.'

'Yes, she did, but dinner these days wouldn't feed
a flea. I tell you, Liam, some nights I could just
scream!'

Liam laughed. 'Don't complain. You're looking
darned good on what your mother's been feeding
you.'

Molly could not stop the flush of pleasure.
'You…you really think so?'

'I really do.' And his eyes were close to admiring as they swept over her new slender figure for the second time that night.

After that, Molly knew she would not eat a morsel.

Fifteen minutes later she was sitting opposite Liam in a booth in one of the cafés along the esplanade and had been fiddling with a large slice of iced carrot cake for a full ten minutes when he finally burst forth.

'I thought you said you were hungry!'

Molly bit her bottom lip and put down the fork. 'I thought I was too. Do you want it?'

He sighed. 'Women! Here, give it to me.'

As she sheepishly handed it over, his exasperation dissolved into a cheeky grin. Molly grinned back, then sat in contented silence to watch Liam eat.

It wasn't long before this innocent enough activity had a less than innocent effect on Molly. Liam's mouth, unfortunately, was incredibly sexy, wide and curving, his full lips saved from outright femininity by the masculine set of his jawline below, and the strong straight nose above. It was also a very mobile mouth, with a very mobile tongue.

Molly's concentration was soon totally on that tongue, and the way its moist pink tip snaked out after every forkful of cake to sweep any crumbs back into his mouth, leaving Liam's lips wet and glistening. Her stomach twisted at the thought of having that tongue-tip do the same to *her* lips, of having it dart between those same lips and slide deep into her waiting, wanting mouth.

Molly smothered a tortured groan and pressed her parched lips firmly together. What she would not give to have that experience…just once.

Regret that she hadn't taken Joan's advice and gone for broke tonight with her appearance rose up to haunt her. Maybe, if she'd left her hair down and worn that perfume, Liam might have found more to admire than her slimmer body. Maybe, if she'd used make-up and worn a sexy scarlet lipstick, he might have been tempted to give her a goodnight kiss.

'Go for it!' Joan had commanded. And what had she done? She'd wimped out. There she'd been, asked out by the man of her dreams, and she'd presented herself to him in clothes her mother would have worn. She was hopeless, absolutely hopeless!

'What's the matter?' Liam asked as he placed his fork across the now empty plate.

Molly was beyond pretending. The eyes she lifted to him were sad eyes. Eyes without hope. She was seeing the end of her dream here.

Liam reached across the table and picked up her left hand. 'Loving this Mr X is making you terribly unhappy, Moll, isn't it?'

Not till today, she accepted with a degree of surprise. Before today, it had been quite a lovely dream. And she *had* had his friendship to sustain her. How many girls did she know who loved lesser men? Unworthy individuals. Creeps, even.

Liam was a man amongst men. He was handsome and clever and essentially good. He loved life, and his mother, and he loved *her,* in a lukewarm brotherly kind of way. Molly could see that now.

'Is there anything I can do to help?' he asked gently, stroking his thumb along the top of her hand all the while.

Molly stiffened under the tinglingly electric feelings it was sending through her. 'I don't think so,' she said tautly. 'It's my problem, and as I said I've decided to move on soon.'

'I think that would be for the best, Moll. Forget this idiot. He doesn't know a good thing when he sees it.'

Molly merely smiled and finally extracted her hand from under his. Liam straightened and studied her with still worried eyes.

'Why don't you do what my mother does when she's down and wants a lift? Go get yourself a new hairstyle. New clothes. New look altogether.'

A bit late for that, she thought, even if I had the money.

But Liam's saying as much piqued her curiosity. 'And what would you suggest?' she asked him. 'I mean, what do you think would suit me?'

Liam laughed. 'Good God, Moll, don't go asking *me.* I have no idea.'

'Liam, you just asked me if you could help, but as soon as I ask something of you you opt out. Look, you're a trained artist, with an eye for design, shape and colour. Think of me as one of your graphic design projects. Pretend you have me up on the screen of your computer, and then make me over to your personal taste and liking.'

'*My* personal taste and liking? Wouldn't it be better if I made you over to Mr X's personal taste and liking?'

'You and he are similar types,' she invented, warming to the game again with each passing moment. Not only that, she was going to take his advice. Whatever Liam suggested she would do, and to hell with the money. She would beg, borrow or steal some, if she had to.

His smile was wry. 'I thought you just said you were moving on.'

'It's a woman's privilege to change her mind.'

Liam shook his head, his eyes wry. 'Somehow I pity this Mr X. He might not know it yet but he's not going to get away easily, is he?'

'Do stop quibbling, Liam. Just give me the once-over and tell me what to change.' She sat up straight and smiled encouragingly at him.

Liam frowned as he looked her over, then shook his head. 'Honestly, Moll, I don't feel at all comfortable with this. You're not a graphic design project. You're a female...with feelings.'

Molly's eyebrows arched. 'Goodness, Liam, that's observant of you. But I shall bravely put aside my feminine sensitivity long enough to hear your unqualified opinion. You said you always admired *my* honesty when I gave you *my* opinion. Now I'm asking for yours.'

He stared at her, still frowning, then shook his head again. 'I'm sorry, Moll, but I really must decline. I suggest you get an expert's opinion.'

'I don't *want* an expert's opinion. I want *yours*. Okay, if you won't tell me straight out, how about we play tick one of the boxes?'

'Tick one of the boxes?'

'Yes. I will suggest a change, then give three possible courses of action. You tell me which one you think will suit me best.'

Liam shrugged. 'If you must. But I won't give any promises or guarantees.'

Molly smiled. 'All care and no responsibility?'

He smiled back. 'Something like that.'

'Fair enough. First thing on the agenda is my hair. I'm going to have it cut. Should I go shoulder-length, jaw-length or really short?'

He tipped his head on one side to consider his answer. 'Really short,' he said at last. 'You have an elegant neck. It's a shame ever to hide it.'

Molly's hand automatically fluttered up to her throat, her stomach curling over at the compliment. She would have to have a good look at her neck when she got home.

'What…what about colour?' she finally went on, hoping she wasn't blushing. 'What do you think would suit me best? Blonde, brunette or redhead?'

'Why don't you just leave it the colour it is?'

'No way! I've lived with mousy brown long enough, thank you very much. There's going to be nothing mousy about me from now on, I can tell you! Now choose!'

Liam sighed. 'Okay, but be it on your head.'

'Well, it will be, won't it?'

He shook his head at her. 'First sarcasm. Now a savage wit. What next?'

Molly crossed her arms on the table. 'Blonde? Brunette? Or redhead?'

'Hmm. Well, you have that fair delicate skin usually associated with redheads, but please...not one of those harsh reds. A rich copper colour would be nice.'

'A rich copper colour,' she repeated, swallowing nervously. Somehow she just couldn't see herself with short red hair. Good God, this was going to take some courage, but she was determined.

Molly opened her mouth to ask Liam about make-up, then shut it again. A man wouldn't know much about that. She would have to consult an expert, maybe in the cosmetics section of a department store.

She began totting-up the cost so far. A top hairdresser. A dye job, which would need retouching every six to eight weeks. New make-up. Not to mention a new wardrobe. Goodness, the mind boggled!

'What about clothes?' she continued. 'I mean...what kind of clothes do you like a girl to wear? Of course I do realise I don't have a spectacular figure like Roxy, but I'm not too bad these days.'

'Don't underestimate yourself, Moll,' he said brusquely. 'I've been noticing tonight what a good little figure you have—one which you seem to have hidden successfully for years. You have a more than adequate bust, a shapely bottom and a nice little waist. You also have remarkably good legs for such a short girl.'

A shocked delight rippled through Molly. Joan had said she had a good figure, but hearing Liam say so was wonderful! And to think all he could find to criticise was her height.

'Unfortunately, Liam,' she said, 'there's nothing I can do about being short. I would dearly love to be taller, believe me.'

'Your Mr X is tall, then?'

'Fairly. And he really likes tall girls.'

'Stupid man. Doesn't he know good things come in small parcels?' He sounded decidedly irritable. 'I suppose you could always wear higher heels than what you have on. You could also give the illusion of further height by shortening your skirts.'

'I have no intention of going to work every day in five-inch heels and minis!'

He gave her a long, hard look. 'You see this Mr X at work, do you?'

'Er...not very often.'

'Then what you wear to work is irrelevant. What you wear when he's around is another thing entirely.'

'If I go to the trouble and expense of all these changes, Liam,' she said firmly, 'then it won't be for Mr X. It will be for me.'

'Sure, Moll, sure. By the way, I don't like stripes,

checks or floral prints. I like my women in figure-hugging clothes in strong block colours.'

When Molly gave him a blank look, he smiled a drily amused smile. 'You said Mr X would have similar tastes to me. Please don't go on pretending this isn't for him. It insults my intelligence.'

'All right. I won't insult your intelligence. Go on. What else don't you like?'

'I don't like girls to wear pants.'

Molly gaped at him. 'If you think I'm going to swan around without my underwear on, then you have another think coming!'

His expression was droll. 'Pants, Moll. Not panties. I'm talking about slack suits, or trousers, if you will.'

'Oh...'

'I don't mind tights. Or jeans, provided they fit well. Men are attracted to a woman's shape. They like to see it.'

'You're a sexist, do you know that?'

The corner of his mouth lifted in a wickedly attractive smile. 'Yes. I like sex. Very much. Is that what you mean by sexist?'

'No. And you darned well know it!'

He looked at her for a long time before speaking. 'Do you like sex, Moll?'

She went bright red. 'I think that's a very personal question.'

'Not really. It's just a general one. I'm not asking for a blow-by-blow description of every sexual experience you've had.'

'Well, if you did, it would be a mighty short conversation,' she snapped. 'In fact, I wouldn't have to say a word!'

He just stared at her. 'Are you saying what I think you're saying?' he asked at last in hushed tones.

His obvious shock infuriated her, as did her having blurted out the awful truth. But she wasn't about to go all shy and embarrassed on him. Pride demanded she hold her head high.

'Really, Liam, there's no need to whisper,' she said coolly. 'I'm not ashamed of my virginity.'

'But you're twenty-*five*, Moll!'

'So what? Is there a prescribed date for such dubious milestones? Where is it written in stone that a girl must lose her virginity before such and such a date? I happen to be waiting for someone special. I didn't want to throw it away on some fumbling boy down behind the school gym, or in the back of a car after a disco. And don't think I haven't had any offers,' she lied. 'Because I have!'

Liam's blue eyes darkened. 'You're waiting for this Mr X, aren't you?'

'And if I am? What's it to you?'

He seemed taken back, then almost outraged. 'You're my best friend, damn it. I don't want to see you hurt.'

Molly was touched, and terribly close to tears. It was a struggle to retain her composure and sense of proportion. If nothing else, she'd made up her mind tonight to do something about changing her dreary

appearance. On top of that, her friendship with Liam
had subtly shifted onto a deeper plane, more like that
of true best friends. There was something very intimate and bonding about sharing confidences.

So now he knew she was a virgin. It was not such
a disaster. How could the truth hurt?

'I'll be all right, Liam,' she said, and actually
reached out to touch *his* hand in a comforting gesture.
'Please don't worry about me and Mr X. Just promise
me you'll be there…when and if I need you.'

She looked deep into his eyes and was moved by
the sincerity of the affection for her she saw there. 'I
think you'd better take me home now,' she said softly.
'Tomorrow's a working day.'

CHAPTER FIVE

JOAN grabbed her the moment she walked into the library, and dragged her down to the privacy of the back room.

'I'm dying of curiosity,' she said, quite unnecessarily, since her whole body language reeked of a breathless tension. 'Did you doll yourself up like I told you to? Did you wear the perfume? Did you knock glamour boy for six when he came to pick you up?'

Molly had thought about what she would tell Joan this morning. She'd walked more slowly to work than usual, mulling over whether she should lie or not. Now the moment of truth was at hand, and despite Joan's eager face Molly could not bring herself to make up a story.

'No, I didn't doll myself up,' she confessed, with a wealth of apology in her voice. 'I didn't wear the perfume, either, though it was a lovely thought, Joan, and I do thank you for it. And as I'm sure you've guessed...no, I didn't knock Liam for six when he came to pick me up.'

Joan exhaled a huge sigh of disappointment. 'Oh, Molly! How many chances like that do you think you're going to get?'

'Actually, last night wasn't a total disaster. Liam did notice at last how much weight I'd lost. He also told me I had a nice figure and good legs...for someone so short.'

'He *did*? Wow! You must have been thrilled to bits.'

'It's not quite as good as it sounds,' Molly said ruefully, then went on to tell Joan exactly how the compliments had come about. She listened intently, her eyes rounding further with each new revelation.

'You mean he thinks you're in love with someone else? This chap he dubbed Mr X?'

'Uh-huh.'

'And he told you how to dress so that you would be more attractive for another man?'

Molly nodded.

'I'd like to strangle him with my bare hands!'

'Don't blame Liam. I forced him into it.'

'Rubbish. The man's a blind fool. Oh, poor Molly!'

'Not "poor Molly" at all, Joan,' she returned with a very firm resolve. 'Because I'm going to do it. Follow all of Liam's suggestions. But not for him. I'm going to do it for myself.'

'Go on with you! You're not!'

'Yes, I am.'

'You're going to cut your hair short and dye it red?'

'For starters. So do you happen to know a good hairdresser who doesn't cost the earth? Also where I might find a make-up expert who gives free advice and tuition?'

Joan's dark eyes twinkled with excitement. 'I certainly do. But gosh, Molly, whatever is your mother going to say?'

Molly wasn't sure. But she would find out that evening. To be honest, the prospect was a daunting one. It wasn't like her to make waves. Or to do something as bold as this.

But she was determined to change herself, and her life…whatever the cost.

Fortunately, she had three hundred dollars put away for emergencies—and which she would use for her first visit to the hairdresser, and some make-up. Still, if she was to find enough money from their tight budget for regular visits to the hairdresser and a whole new wardrobe, then some more changes would have to be made to their day-to-day lifestyle.

Her own salary was almost totally eaten up with the two mortgages her father had taken out shortly before he died, and her mother's pension barely covered their living expenses and other bills, with little left over for luxuries.

Molly waited till after dinner before she brought up her plans for her future, and was not really surprised when her mother reacted badly.

'But *why* do you want to change yourself so dramatically?' Ruth asked in a tremulous voice. 'I don't understand. This isn't like you at all!'

'Mum,' Molly returned patiently, 'I'm twenty-five and I have not had one single steady boyfriend in my life. I do not want to become an old maid. I want to get married one day and have a family of my own. To get married I need a man, and to get a man I need to do something about attracting one.'

'It's not *any* man you want to attract, missie,' came her waspish accusation. 'It's Liam Delaney. You were perfectly happy till you went out with him last night and now you've got all these silly ideas in your head.'

'They are not silly ideas,' Molly said more sternly. 'Yes, I do have feelings for Liam. I always have had. I won't deny it. But you were right when you said he'd never fall in love with me. He thinks of me as a kid sister. But that doesn't mean I'm going to spend the rest of my life pining for him. Since men don't exactly come flocking to my door, I aim to get out and about a bit more, and I aim to look darned good when I do so. Looking good costs money, which brings me to my first suggestion. What do you think about selling this house and buying something smaller? The mortgages are killing us.'

Her mother gave her a truly horrified look. 'Oh, no. No, no, no! I love this house. It's all I have. You can't ask that of me. You can't!'

Molly relented and moved straight on to plan B. To be honest she hadn't really wanted to sell. As much as she'd told both Joan and her mother that these radical changes were for herself, she still wanted to see Liam's reaction to the finished product. Silly of her perhaps, but a fact.

'Okay, forget selling,' she said briskly. 'My alternative suggestion is that we advertise for a boarder.'

'A boarder!'

'Yes. We have four bedrooms in this house, Mum, two of which are never used, the master bedroom being one of them. You could get good money for that room. It has an *en suite,* a dressing room and lots of space.'

'Oh, but I couldn't have some strange man living in your father's house and sleeping in his bed!'

Molly prayed for more patience. Her mother's devotion to her father had increased considerably since his death. Couldn't she remember what a selfish bastard he'd been? How he'd wasted all her inheritance from her parents on one of his stupid get-rich schemes? Worst of all, how he'd often come home late, smelling of booze and cheap perfume?

'You don't have to have a male boarder, Mum. I'm sure there are plenty of widows around your age who need accommodation. It would be company for you as well,' Molly pointed out. 'I'm not going to be at home quite as much as I used to be.'

Ruth opened her mouth to protest again, then closed it, her expression petulant. She looked like a sulky child sitting there. Molly felt sorry for her but knew she had to make a stand or her future would be as dull and dreary as she'd been fearing.

'Do I have your agreement to put an ad in next Wednesday's paper?'

'I won't have anyone I don't like.'

'Of course not.'

Ruth gave her daughter another resentful look. 'So how much money is it that you want to spend on yourself?'

'Not as much as I first estimated. Joan's put me on to a local lady who does hair from her home and is very reasonable. And she says the make-up department at the David Jones store at Tuggerah will give me good free advice on making up my face properly. Still, a reasonably good make-up range could run to a couple of hundred dollars. I have enough rainy-day money put by for that, but I will still need to save at least a hundred dollars a week for a while so that I can get together a decent wardrobe of both casual and dressy clothes. Luckily, I wear a uniform to work, so that's not a problem.'

'Next thing you'll be wanting to get a driving licence and buy a car!'

Molly accepted her mother's caustic outburst, disarming her with a sweet smile. 'I hadn't thought of it but that's a very good idea. Thank you for mentioning it, Mum. I'll definitely put that on my list for future projects, along with a South Seas cruise. Now I think I'll go upstairs and have a nice long bath. My legs are aching from standing up all day. Oh, and Mum, do you think I might have a bit more for dinner at night? I'm going to need a lot more energy in the not too distant future.' And she swept from the kitchen, leaving her mother to gape after her.

* * *

'I can't believe it's me!' Molly exclaimed delightedly. 'You're a genius, Leanne!'

The hairdresser's smile carried a delicious satisfaction. 'I must admit I have outdone myself this time.'

Molly beamed anew at this striking and sophisticated-looking creature who was staring back at her in the mirror. She turned her head from side to side and watched the smooth coppery cap shimmer and sway, then fall perfectly back into place.

'This particular cut will give your hair body and style,' Leanne had pronounced reassuringly while she proceeded to shape and shave Molly's hair around her ears and at the back, while layering the top in concentric circles from the crown.

Molly now had a stylish fringe right down to her eyebrows, the effect being to diminish the size of her nose and highlight her wide, deeply set green eyes. The new coppery colour, besides being eye-catching in itself, was a perfect foil for her pale skin, giving it a translucency and delicacy which had been lost against her mousy brown hair.

When Molly stood up she saw delightedly that the clean lines made her neck look longer and even more elegant.

'You really look different,' the hairdresser said, shaking her head admiringly. 'Taller, too.'

'Yes, I think you're right,' Molly agreed excitedly. 'Oh, Leanne, how can I ever thank you? And it was so kind of you to fit me in tonight.'

'It was my pleasure. Now, how are you going to

get home?' Leanne asked once Molly had handed over the money.

'Oh, I'll walk. It's not far.' Leanne lived less than a block from the library, which was only a fifteen-minute walk from her house.

Leanne frowned. 'Do you think that's wise? It's Friday night, you know.'

'What do you mean?'

'People let their hair down on a Friday night around here. You'll have to walk past the tavern on your way home, won't you?'

'Yes.'

'Then watch yourself. You're not exactly inconspicuous with that new red hair, you know.'

Leanne's warning startled Molly. She'd never been hassled by unwanted male attention in all her life and simply could not anticipate that a mere change in hair colour would create trouble for her, especially when she was still dressed in her library uniform.

But she was wrong.

She'd just passed the tavern and was halfway along the flat stretch which followed the railway line when a hotted-up Chevie full of some less than savoury individuals rumbled by.

'Hey, babe,' one of them called out.

Molly averted her eyes and crossed the road as soon as they passed by, then nearly died when she heard the tyres screech as the driver executed a U-turn. Before she could blink, the car was cruising along next to her and an obviously drunk, loud-mouthed lout was leaning out of the passenger window in her direction.

'Where's yuh goin', honey?' he said, breathing beer fumes her way. 'Wanna ride?'

She quickened her step and kept her eyes straight ahead.

'Whatsa matter? You think you're too good for us? She thinks she's too good for us, fellas. What do yuh reckon? Do yuh think we should teach Madam Muck a lesson or two?'

Her mouth dry with fear, Molly was just about to run for it when a sleek black car shot around the Chevie and pulled up dead. The driver of the Chevie had to brake hard to avoid a collision and the lout hanging out of the window almost tipped out onto the road. When a really big dark-haired man dressed in black jumped out from behind the wheel of the black car and began stalking back towards Molly's verbal assailant, the lout shouted something and scrambled back into the car. The Chevie reversed like mad, spun round and roared off.

Her saviour curved his big hands over her shaking shoulders and peered down into her ashen face. 'You all right, little lady?' he asked.

It was only then that Molly recognised the identity of her rescuer.

It was Dennis Taylor.

'Yes, I think so,' came her weakly breathless answer. 'Thanks so much for stopping, Dennis.'

His surprise at her knowing his name was obvious

in the jerking back of his head, and the widening of his dark eyes.

Molly would have been gratified if she hadn't still been shaking like a leaf. 'It's Molly,' she said. 'Molly McCrae.'

'Molly?' His startled gaze lifted to her hair, then swiftly ran down her body and up again. 'Good Lord, so it is. I didn't recognise you with that stunning hair. And you've lost weight too, haven't you?'

'A little.'

His smile took on a knowing edge as he looked her up and down again. 'More than a little. You're looking fantastic. Too fantastic to be walking around these streets at night on your own. No wonder you almost got yourself into trouble. Come on, I'll drive you home.'

After her frightening experience with those creeps, Molly wasn't about to refuse. She wouldn't have been human, either, if she hadn't been flattered by Dennis's compliments on her appearance, and by the way he kept looking at her.

His touch seemed gentle and solicitous as he helped her into the passenger side of his roomy black sedan, but when he sashed the seat belt into place for her Molly was quite sure his left hand deliberately brushed over the tips of her breasts. She stiffened inside but said nothing, ignoring his attempt to make eye contact at the same time.

Creeps came in various forms, she realised ruefully. Dennis wasn't much different from those louts. His approach was different, that was all. No doubt he didn't go in for outright rape. Silky smooth seductions and one-night stands would be more his forte. He would use his silver tongue to talk his way into a girl's bed. Molly decided not to get too carried away with Dennis's words of praise. She didn't doubt she looked better with her new hairdo, but she wasn't competition for Roxy just yet.

They were only a minute away from her home by car. But Dennis didn't waste a second, bombarding her with questions designed to elicit the only information from a female he would want to know. How old was she exactly? Where did she work these days? Did she have a boyfriend? Unfortunately, Molly didn't realise where Dennis was heading till she'd told him several truths with naive honesty.

As soon as he pulled up at the kerb outside her house, he turned and asked her if she'd like to come out with him for a drink later that night.

'I could pick you up at…say…around ten-thirty?'

Molly might have been inexperienced with men but she knew that to agree to such an invitation at that hour of the night was to agree to more than a drink. She didn't doubt she'd *get* a drink. Plenty of them. And all of them alcoholic. Then, when she was suitably plastered, Dennis would take her back to his orgy palace for a night of raw naked sex.

The very thought of Dennis naked made her want to retch. Facially he was quite handsome, if you liked Mediterranean-looking men with thick wiry black hair and a permanent five o'clock shadow. But his body was humungous in size. And hairy. Like a big gorilla.

No doubt a lot of women fancied his darkly macho appearance, but Molly preferred Liam's fairer, more elegant looks. Her favourite fantasy always included running her hands through his silky blond locks and over his smooth, hairless chest. It turned her on just to *imagine* touching his body, whereas the thought of touching Dennis made her skin crawl.

'Thank you, Dennis,' she said politely. 'For everything. But I'm sorry, I can't. Not tonight.'

To give him credit he took rejection well. Maybe, because of his salesman's training, he did not regard anyone saying no on a first occasion as rejection, but as merely a challenge, for his black eyes glittered with undeniable confidence as he smiled over at her.

'That's all right. Another time maybe?'

'Perhaps,' she replied, not wanting to be too rude after his kindness in rescuing her.

'I'll call you,' he said, and restarted the engine.

Molly could see she was expected to let herself out. Maybe Dennis didn't take rejection so well after all.

She waited till he had driven off, then turned to walk along the front path. An upward glance showed the light on in the bedroom her mother now occupied. Molly wasn't looking forward to showing her mother the result of the first stage of her make-over. But there was no getting around it. Better she get it over with tonight.

'I'm home!' she called out as she came into the house.

No answer.

Her heartbeat quickening with nerves, she locked the door behind her then trudged on up the stairs and tapped on her mother's door. 'Can I come in?'

A down-in-the-mouth 'I suppose so' finally filtered through the door.

Molly would always remember the look on her mother's face when she first entered the room.

'Well, you've really done it now, haven't you?' Ruth snapped. 'Gone and cut off all your lovely long hair and had it dyed a cheap brassy red. Don't expect me to say I like it, Molly, because I don't. I'm sorry, but I'm not going to lie.'

It saddened Molly that her mother was not only *not* sorry at all, but she *had* lied. For the truth had rocketed from her momentarily rounded eyes before she'd been able to hide it.

Her new hairstyle *was* fantastic, as both Leanne and Dennis had said. And so was the colour. Fantastic and flattering!

Molly generously put her mother's negative reaction down to insecurity over her daughter's belatedly spreading her wings. It could not be jealousy. Surely not!

'That's all right, Mum,' she said with determined cheerfulness. 'You don't have to like it. *I* do. And I'm pleased to announce it's already an unqualified success where the opposite sex is concerned, which is the name of the game, isn't it?'

'What?' Ruth sat up straighter against her pillows. 'You're saying Liam's seen you already? I didn't know he was home for the weekend. I didn't see his car outside.'

'Not Liam, Mum. Dennis.'

'Dennis? Dennis who?'

'Dennis Taylor. You know Dennis Taylor, Mum. Well, he saw me walking home and gave me a lift. He said my hair looked fantastic. He even asked me out.'

'Asked you out? Dennis Taylor asked you out?'

'That's what I said.'

'You...you didn't say you would go, did you, Molly?'

'Not this time,' came her airy reply. 'But that was because I was too tired. I'm sure he'll ask again. Meanwhile, I think I'll go to bed. I have a busy day tomorrow, what with make-up to buy and lots of lovely clothes to look at and try on. See you in the morning, Mum.' And, after giving her a goodnight peck, Molly whirled round and walked from the room.

CHAPTER SIX

MOLLY was practising her daytime make-up routine the following Sunday morning when the telephone rang.

'Can you answer that, Mum?' she called out.

There was no reply and the phone kept on ringing. Molly suddenly remembered that her mother had gone down to the corner store to buy the Sunday papers. Carefully, she put down her new mascara wand then hurried downstairs to sweep up the receiver.

'Hi there,' she said breezily.

'Molly? Is that you?'

Her heart caught at the sound of Liam's voice, reminding her forcibly how much she loved this man. The realisation wrenched her momentarily out of her newly found optimism, bringing her down to earth with a thud. But then she regathered herself, her spirits lifting with the thought that Liam was actually calling her. That was a first!

'It certainly is me, Liam. Don't I sound like me?'

'Actually no...you sound different, somehow.'

'Really?' I *look* different too, she was tempted to add, but didn't want to spoil the surprise when he eventually saw her in the flesh. 'Sorry. It's just the same little old me,' she went on, smiling to herself.

Her height was one thing she simply could not change. Though the four-inch heels she'd tried on yesterday and which she would buy shortly certainly gave her a taller view of the world. 'So to what do I owe the dubious honour of your call?'

'Are you being sarcastic?'

Molly chuckled at the shocked tone of his question. 'Who, me? Never!'

'Have you been drinking?'

Now he sounded almost churlish.

'*This* early on a Sunday morning?' It was five past ten. 'Which brings me to a repeat of *my* question. Why are you calling me?'

'What? Oh, I um…I'm on my way up to help Mum move some furniture around. She's decided she's bored with the layout in the living rooms. Actually, I think it's just an excuse to get me home and feed me up. Anyway, I thought of you saying the other night that you don't get fed properly at home, and I was wondering if you'd like to join us for lunch.'

'Join you for lunch,' she repeated, swallowing convulsively and immediately going blank.

'You don't have to sound so thrilled,' came his testy remark. 'I realise I'm not your Mr X but I've always thought you enjoyed my company.'

'Oh, but I do!' she hastened to assure him. 'I mean, I…I…'

'You have something else on? Is that it?'

Molly tried to pull herself together. It was the shock, that was all. She glanced in the wall mirror above the telephone table and nerves immediately besieged her. Would Liam think she looked fantastic when he saw her? Might he be inspired to ask her out on a date, like Dennis had? A *real* date?

'No, nothing else on,' she said at last. 'And I'd love to join you and your mother for lunch. Would you like me to help you move the furniture as well?'

'Would you?'

'Love to. Make-overs are my thing this week.'

'What?'

'Nothing,' she muttered, and wished she were more confident of Liam's reaction to her own make-over.

'I'll see you in about fifteen minutes, then. Just come over when you see my car.'

'But…but…'

'Look, I'm ringing from my mobile and I'd better hang up before I get into trouble.'

He hung up and Molly groaned into the dead receiver. Fifteen minutes. Oh, God…

With a squawk, she dropped the receiver back into place and dashed upstairs, throwing open her wardrobe and searching for something Liam might like. No pants, she reminded herself, and passed over the cheap tights and tracksuit pants she lived in around the house. Her eyes went to the lime-green T-shirt she'd bought the previous day, the only item of clothing she could afford with the fifteen dollars she'd had left over after her skin-care and make-up splurge. It was one of the 'in' colours of the season and suited her new vibrant hair colour.

But she had nothing to go with it.

In despair, she pulled on a pair of cream Bermuda shorts which, though bought two years back when she'd been larger, had an elastic waistline and didn't look too bad. Didn't look too good either, but, darn it all, it was too hot for jeans and she didn't have enough time to find anything else. Ten minutes had flown by since Liam had called.

Shoving her feet into tan sandals, Molly spun round to the dressing-table to finish her make-up, but her hands were shaking so badly she had to abandon applying mascara. Fortunately, she'd already done her eyeshadow and eyeliner, adding enough depth and definition to her eyes for casual daytime wear. Her foundation, blusher and translucent powder were also in place, covering up the smattering of freckles across her nose and cheeks. All that was left to do was her lipstick.

She'd bought two new lipsticks the day before. Bronze and Flame, both in a stayfast brand. She hated lip-prints left on cups and glasses. Neither did she want to become one of those females who had to touch up their make-up all the time. All the make-up she'd purchased was supposed to stay all day—and all night if necessary.

This last thought sent Molly's pulse racing. There was only one man she'd want to wake up with in the morning, with her make-up still intact.

Somehow, the bronze-coloured lipstick found its proper place without wandering all over her face. A quick brush of her hair, several deep, steadying breaths and she was ready. Just in time, too, for when she leant across her bed to glance through her bedroom window she was greeted by the sight of Liam's new red car coming up the hill.

Her stomach tightened another notch, her heart pounding. One last glance at her baggy shorts brought a grimace and another flicker of doubt. The last thing Molly needed at that moment was to come downstairs and be met with her mother's open scorn.

Ruth walked in the front door just as Molly approached it. 'And where do you think you're off to with your face all done up like a dog's dinner? No, you don't have to tell me. I can guess. I saw his car pass by as I walked up the hill, and you're running straight over to parade yourself in front of him. Dear heaven, but you're a fool, Molly McCrae. That girlfriend of his would still run rings around you for looks and style. You can tart yourself up all you like and it won't make a blind bit of difference. Not where *Liam* is concerned. Of course there are *other* men around here who aren't so particular. Not that they ever *marry* the girls they ask out.'

For a few seconds, Molly's confidence in her appearance wavered. But she'd come too far to allow anyone to undermine her newly found self-esteem. Not that her mother's nasty comments hadn't hurt.

'Maybe I'm not in Roxy's league in the looks department, Mum,' she said, her voice shaking with emotion. 'But I still think I look pretty good. And I'll have you know I'm not running over there to parade myself in front of Liam. He rang me while you were out and asked me over for lunch. It seems he and Roxy have broken up. Maybe I don't stand a chance with him, Mum, but that's no excuse for your trying to put me down like that. It was mean.'

To give her credit, her mother looked shocked, then stricken with remorse. 'Oh, Molly... I... I... Oh, dear. Oh, I'm so sorry. I... I just don't want to see you hurt...'

'Then stop *hurting* me,' she countered, sweeping out of the house before her mother could say another word, anger propelling her down the front path. As she stalked out onto the roadway and turned right, Molly indulged in some none too ladylike mutterings.

'My, my,' drawled a male voice. 'Does that brand-new temper come with the brand-new hair?'

Molly scudded to a ragged halt, her eyes whipping up to see Liam leaning against his open car door, watching her. His eyes immediately narrowed on her newly made-up face, then lifted to once again take in her new crowning glory. She couldn't tell if he approved of her transformation or not.

'You...you don't like it?' she almost groaned after a few seconds' silence, one hand flying up to touch her hair in that age-old feminine gesture which invited more reassurance.

Liam straightened and slammed the car door before glaring back her way. 'Don't be ridiculous. What's not to like? You look fantastic. But I think you know that, don't you?'

Molly glared back at him. So much for Liam being bowled over by her sudden beauty!

'I only did what you suggested the other night,' she defended hotly.

'True. But I honestly never expected you to do it. I guess I underestimated the power of your Mr X. So...has he seen the new you yet?'

Molly bristled, then lifted her small chin to look Liam straight in the eye. 'Yes, he has, as a matter of a fact.'

'I suppose he said you looked fantastic.'

Once again, Molly was spurred on to play an ironic game with the truth. Somehow, it soothed the pain of Liam's ongoing blindness. How could he not guess? she agonised inside. Couldn't he see her love for him in her desperate desire for his approval? 'Actually, they were his exact words,' she tossed back coolly.

His frown was instant. 'Where is it that you see this...Don Juan?' he demanded to know.

Molly smiled a darkly devious smile. It amused her that Mr X didn't find favour with Liam. If only he knew!

'Oh, he lives nearby, and I run into him from time to time. But, as I said before, my love life is really none of your business, is it? Now, shouldn't we be going inside to help your mother with the furniture?' she went on with more forcefulness than was usually her nature. 'Time is a-wasting, you know, and I have to get back to practising my new make-up before the working week begins. I aim to knock their socks off tomorrow morning.'

He threw her an incredulous glance, then shook his head. 'They say women change their personalities when they change their hair colour. I'm beginning to believe it.'

'Oh? Did you know Roxy before she peroxided her hair? Was she a sweet little thing before she became a bottle-blonde?'

'We're not discussing Roxy here, Miss Sarcasm. Which is exactly the sort of thing I'm referring to. You were never one to be bitchy before. Neither did you go round swearing under your breath.'

'Maybe you just never heard me before. Maybe you don't know the real me at all, Liam. Maybe you've never stopped to smell the flowers.'

'Stopped to smell the flowers? What in hell has my stopping to smell the flowers got to do with your turning into a shrew?'

Molly laughed while Liam scowled. It was at that moment his mother opened her front door and came out onto the porch to stare over at both of them.

Babs Delaney was a handsome woman. Somewhere in her late fifties, she was tall and slender, with intelligent blue eyes and streaky ash-blonde hair which fell to her shoulders in a stylish bob. Unlike her son she obviously liked women in trousers for she lived in them. Today she was wearing a loose pair of fawn cotton trousers with a bright floral floaty overblouse.

A pair of reading glasses hung on a gold chain around her neck.

She lifted a hand to shade her eyes from the sunlight, squinting down at this strange young woman with her son. Molly smiled with satisfaction when she realised Liam's mother didn't recognise her.

'Hi there, Mum.' Liam waved. 'Be right with you. Moll here's going to help us.'

'Moll?' his mother repeated, frowning.

Liam sighed his exasperation. 'Oh, all right. I'll call her Molly in your presence, if you insist. I can't understand why you have such an aversion to nicknames when you go by the moniker of Babs. Come on, *Molly*.'

'Molly?' Babs stared as Liam guided her up his front steps. 'Oh, my goodness, it's *Molly*! From next door!'

'Yes, it's Molly from next door,' Liam said as he pecked his mother on the cheek, then threw Molly a dry look over his shoulder. 'In a fashion...'

'I'm so sorry, Molly, dear,' Liam's mother directed at Molly with an apologetic smile. 'I didn't recognise you with that stunning new hair colour and style. My, but it suits her, doesn't it, Liam? She looks a different girl entirely.'

'She does indeed,' Liam said in a tone which had his mother raising her eyebrows at him before turning to take Molly's arm.

'Who did it for you, dear?' she asked as she led

her inside. 'I'm always on the lookout for a good hairdresser.'

They stopped together in the tiled foyer while Molly raved on about Leanne's abilities and moderate prices, till Liam finally interrupted. 'Have I come home to move furniture or not?'

'Don't be rude, dear,' Babs told him dismissively. 'The furniture can wait. It's not going anywhere. I'll just go put on the jug and catch up with Molly here for a bit. I haven't had a good talk to her in ages. Remember when she used to come over every Sunday, Liam, and you would make her sit in your room all afternoon while you showed her whatever game you were working on that week? I used to think she deserved a medal for how patient she was with you. And how kind. Not too many girls her age would have bothered being friends with an egocentric computer nut like you, dear.'

'I didn't mind, Mrs Delaney,' Molly confessed. 'Truth is I enjoyed it though I can't say I always understood everything. Liam's nothing short of a creative genius. I dare say he gets that from you.'

Babs smiled her pleasure at the compliment. 'What a nice girl you are,' she said. 'But my son is no genius. Not in the things which count, that is,' she muttered as she turned to walk down several steps into the sunken living areas of the house.

Liam's home was roomy, split-level and messy, Molly saw as she traipsed after Liam's mother. And it smelt like a tavern. Housework was clearly not a priority with Mrs Delaney. Funny. Molly couldn't remember it being so unkempt in the old days.

She and Liam followed his mother through the large family room into a kitchen which would have given her own mother an instant nervous breakdown. Molly had never seen so many piles of dirty dishes in her life!

'Sorry about the mess,' Babs Delaney excused with an unconcerned but elegant wave of her right hand. 'My cleaner had to quit through ill health a couple of weeks back and I'm on a deadline for a book. I've been meaning to advertise for a replacement but haven't got around to it.'

An idea popped into Molly's mind. 'How much does a cleaner earn?'

'What?'

Molly repeated the question.

'Oh, I'm not sure what the going rate is. I paid my lady fifty dollars a day cash in hand,' Babs replied as she angled the kettle under the tap. A difficult task, under the circumstances, since the sink was full. 'She used to come in on Mondays and Fridays for six hours a time. Still, she did do all the washing and ironing as well as the cleaning, and any extra jobs I needed done, so she was well worth every penny. It left me totally free to write, which meant I earned more money in the long run.'

'I see,' Molly murmured thoughtfully.

Liam's mother slanted her a sharp look. 'Do you know someone who might be interested?'

Molly hesitated. 'I might...'

'Your mother?' Babs guessed, turning to put the kettle on the counter and plug it in.

'Well...yes. Dad left her with a lot of debts, you see, and her pension doesn't go far. I suggested that we take in a boarder to help make ends meet better, but I don't think Mum liked that idea much.'

'Why don't I go ask her, then, right now?' Babs offered. 'And while I'm at it I'll ask her over to lunch with us. I've got plenty of food. Meanwhile, Liam, load up the dishwasher for me, like a good boy, will you? If Molly's mother's house is anything like her garden then she'll be horrified at the state of this place. Molly, love, would you mind collecting the dirty glasses from the living room? Oh, and the ashtrays as well? I had some visitors over last night who smoked like chimneys.'

Molly was happy to. What a nice lady Liam's mother was! As soon as Babs left, she whizzed around the living room, straightening it up a bit while Liam made clattering noises in the kitchen. When she came out at last with four dirty glasses and a stack of ashtrays to empty hc had just closed the dishwasher door and started the cycle.

'I'll wash these up in the sink,' she said, and set to work straight way.

Liam leant against a nearby counter, his arms crossed and his eyes thoughtful upon her. 'When you say your father left debts behind, just how much debt do you mean?'

'A lot,' Molly admitted. 'The year before he died, he took out loans against the house to finance his latest business venture, which went bust like every other one of his get-rich-quick schemes. Unfortunately there was no life insurance to cover these loans. The repayments take nearly all my salary each week.'

Liam straightened, his expression appalled. 'But that's terrible! Why didn't you tell me about this sooner?'

'Why should I have? It's not your problem, Liam.'

'Some best friend you must think I am,' he said sharply.

Molly was astonished by his annoyance. 'But I... I...'

'I want you to tell me exactly who these loans are with and what interest you're paying.'

'Why?'

'Because I want to help you, that's why.'

'Help me how?'

'That depends.'

'On what?'

'On how much stupid pride you've got.'

Her chin shot up. 'I have quite a bit. And I don't think pride is at all stupid!'

'That's what I thought, so I could do one of two things. I could have my accountant look at these loans and see what is the best way to refinance them at the lowest possible interest. Men like your father always have to borrow at exorbitant interest rates because they're a credit risk. On top of that, interest rates have dropped lately. Alternatively, I could organise to pay off the debts myself by giving you an interest-free loan. We could draw up a legal document to satisfy your pride. Either way, your repayments would be substantially less than they are now.'

Molly's face lit up. 'An interest-free loan! Oh, Liam, that would be wonderful! Simply wonderful!' But then her face fell. 'But they're not my debts. In a legal sense, that is. They're Mum's. She would have to sign any documents. And I don't think she would agree to your last suggestion. I mean...she might think it was...funny.'

'What do you mean...funny?'

'She might think there were strings attached to such an arrangement.'

'Strings? What kind of strings?'

'Liam, don't be thick, please. Between you and me.'

Liam's shock was not altogether flattering. 'She thinks I would demand you sleep with me in exchange for money? Why in God's name would she think such a thing?'

Molly could hardly tell him the truth—that it was her daughter Ruth believed capable of bad things where Liam was concerned, not the other way around. Still, she had to say something. Liam was clearly offended by the implication that he was the type of man who would blackmail, or bribe, a girl into bed.

'Don't take it personally. Mum doesn't have a great opinion of men in general when it comes to sex,

Liam,' she said. 'Dad was an inveterate womaniser, you know.'

'No,' he said slowly, that frown still in place. 'I didn't know. You never told me. You never told me anything much about yourself or your family.' Now he was sounding frustrated.

'You never asked.'

'Well, I'm asking now!'

'Why?'

'Why?'

'Yes, why this sudden interest?'

Liam was taken aback, then thoroughly exasperated. 'Why must women make mountains out of molehills? There's no mystery to my interest. Neither is it *sudden*. I've always cared about you, Molly, but I guess I've been so wrapped up in myself and getting my business going that I haven't had much time to think of other people's problems. I suggest you put this change of heart down to my maturing at long last, if you have to put it down to anything. I did turn thirty this year.'

'Yes, I know,' she said drily. 'I bought *and* lit the candles on your cake.'

'You still haven't forgiven me for forgetting your birthday this week, have you?'

'I'll forgive you anything if you have your accountant get me some more money each week. I'm dying to buy myself some lovely new clothes to go with my new look. Believe me, Liam, if you can organise that refinancing business, I'll be your willing slave for ever.' And wasn't *that* the truth, she thought ruefully.

He gave her a decidedly disgruntled look. 'So I'm to be responsible for even *more* changes in my Molly. Your Mr X won't be able to resist you soon. Frankly, I'm not so sure I want to send you into the arms of some good-looking bastard who's had oodles of women and who didn't appreciate the lovely person you were *before* you became a fashion plate.'

Molly was startled, then flattered by the jealous edge in his words. It occurred to her that inventing the mythical Mr X was the best thing she'd ever done. She'd never had so much attention from Liam in her life. Suddenly, she was a reasonably attractive female, complete with a secret sexual obsession. The fact that that sexual obsession was Liam himself might have escaped him, but the concept of her being madly in love with some good-looking Casanova clearly bothered him. Surely that had to be reason to keep hoping?

'I don't think you're in love with this man at all,' Liam pronounced abruptly. 'From what I've heard, it's a simple case of infatuation. When and if he ever takes you to bed, you'll realise that. Men like him rarely live up to the romantic and sexual fantasies women weave around them. They're much too selfish to be good lovers.'

'That's a very interesting theory,' Molly said thoughtfully. 'And do you think you're a good lover, Liam?'

'*Me*? We're not talking about *me*!' he grumbled irritably. 'We're talking about lover boy here.'

'I was just wondering,' she said with feigned innocence. 'After all, you confessed the other day to being selfish. And you just said selfish men weren't good lovers.'

'Yes, well, there's selfish and there's selfish. I like to think I excel in anything I put my mind to. So yes, I think I'm a good lover. Are you going to argue the point, Miss Picky, or accept my word for it?'

Actually, I'd like a demonstration, Molly thought with a quickening of her heartbeat. She stared first into Liam's beautiful blue eyes, then down at his equally beautiful mouth before letting her hopefully unreadable gaze drift down his even more beautiful body.

Her own ached with longing for that body. It was a bittersweet ache, filled with a delicious sexual awareness, yet framed within a frustration so acute, she wanted to scream and shout and stamp her feet.

'I guess I'll have to accept your word for it,' she managed to say, though her words were clipped. 'I certainly won't be ringing Roxy and asking her, that's for sure. The best thing you ever did was to break up with *her*.'

'Break up with Roxy? I haven't broken up with Roxy. Wherever did you get *that* idea?'

'But the other night…you said…'

'I said we were having a trial separation. Actually, it was her idea. She had some bee in her bonnet about my taking her for granted, which was probably true. So she told me she wasn't going to see me for a month, during which we were to have no contact whatsoever, even by telephone.'

'I see.' Molly felt her brave and exciting new world tip out of kilter. 'So when is this month up?' she asked, her voice flat and heavy.

'Next Sunday.' He raked his hands agitatedly through his hair. 'And it can't come soon enough, I can tell you. This has been the longest, most frustrating four weeks in my life!'

CHAPTER SEVEN

AFTER that, nothing could have made Molly happy, not even when Babs returned with her still apologetic-looking mother in tow. Amazingly, Ruth was thrilled by the idea of becoming Mrs Delaney's cleaner, then ecstatic when Liam explained his refinancing offer.

'Isn't that wonderful news, Molly?' her mother exclaimed. 'Now we won't have to have a stranger in the house. And you'll have some money for yourself for a change.'

Molly smiled and said yes, it was wonderful. She smiled all through lunch and laughed when the four of them moved Babs's living-room furniture to new spots, then had to move everything back again to their original places when the end result did not please Babs's creative eye.

No one would have guessed how wretched Molly felt. She was a past master at hiding her feelings, especially around Liam. But her heart grew heavier as the hours passed. By afternoon tea, she was exhausted with the emotional strain of pretending to be bright and breezy when inside she was shattered. Liam's getting back with Roxy the following Sunday was the final straw.

His eagerness for their reconciliation had been palpable, his body language reeking of sexual frustration as he'd spoken of his time away from Roxy. He could not wait to jump back into bed with her. Molly could no longer fool herself. Any attention he'd been giving *her* had been the result of his boredom, not because of any suddenly selfless maturity.

'You won't forget about the refinancing,' she reminded him stiffly when it came time for them to leave.

'Not at all. In fact, Ruth's going to give me the relevant papers this very afternoon. I'll collect them shortly, Ruth, and have Nigel get onto it first thing this week, then I'll bring up whatever needs to be signed next Saturday.'

'You coming home next Saturday, are you?' Molly asked with a weary resignation. Normally, the thought of Liam being around thrilled her to pieces. Now there was no pleasure in the news, only the cynical thought that of course he was coming home. He had nothing better to do till Sunday, did he?

'Yes, I've been invited to speak at a local business awards dinner on Saturday night. I'm also presenting the prizes.'

'How nice,' Molly said blandly.

'Why don't you take Molly, Liam?' his mother suggested. 'The invitation says "and partner".'

Liam's instant frown was enough to turn Molly off the idea, despite her stupid heart giving one last feeble leap. His eyes turned her way then travelled slowly over her. She could actually see his brain ticking away. Dear old Moll doesn't look half bad now. She wouldn't be an embarrassment to take, not like she would have been a week ago.

'Would you like to go?' he asked her. 'It's black tie, so you'll need a dinner dress.'

Molly steeled herself to do the one thing she'd thought she would never do. Reject the man she loved.

'Thank you, Liam,' she said with superb indifference, 'but I have other plans for next Saturday night.'

His blue eyes instantly clouded and a small stab of triumph lifted her spirits momentarily, quickly followed by a much stronger stab of despair. Tears threatened and she just had to get out of there.

Panic had her glancing around for her mother. 'Ready to go home, Mum?' she asked, determined to keep up the false gaiety to the bitter end. 'I have quite a bit to do before the working week starts tomorrow.'

'My working week starts tomorrow too, doesn't it, Babs?' Ruth returned happily.

'Indeed it does.'

'Thank you so much,' Ruth went on, clasping her neighbour's hands with her own with rather touching gratitude. 'For the lunch. And...and everything.'

Babs smiled and patted Ruth's hands. 'It's I who's grateful. I've found myself a wonderful cleaner and a new friend as well. See you in the morning, Ruth.'

'And I'll be seeing you later, Mrs McCrae!' Liam called out as Molly shepherded her mother out of the house. 'To get those papers.'

'What nice people they are,' Ruth said on the short way home. 'And wasn't it kind of Liam to help us out with that money business?'

'Yes, it was,' Molly admitted, but tight-lipped.

A silence descended between the two women as they made their way inside, but Molly could feel her mother watching her.

'Why didn't you say yes when Liam asked you to go out with him?' Ruth asked once they were safely alone in the kitchen. 'It...it wasn't because of what I said earlier, was it? About your not being... well...pretty enough for him? Because that's not true, Molly. You're plenty pretty enough. And he really likes you. I can see that now. He could hardly take his eyes off you all over lunch, and then later when he...'

'Oh, Mum, *please*,' Molly begged. 'You don't have to lie. You were right the first time.'

'No, Molly, I wasn't. I was wrong. Very wrong. And I'm thoroughly ashamed of myself. I was feeling sorry for myself, and I was afraid. Yes, afraid,' she repeated when Molly's eyes widened. 'Afraid some man would snap you up, looking as you do now, and I'd be left all alone in this world.

'But today opened my eyes a lot. There's Babs Delaney, a widow like myself, but she doesn't sit around feeling sorry for herself. Besides her writing, she plays golf and bingo and bridge. And she doesn't try to tie that boy of hers to her apron-strings, either. I can see it's up to me to make something of my life for myself. I know becoming a cleaner isn't much, but at least I'm good at it, and it's a start. I might even go to that hairdresser of yours with some of my cleaning money and become a blonde!'

'Oh, Mum!' Molly exclaimed, a burst of very real joy dragging her heart back out of the doldrums. 'You've no idea how happy you've made me, hearing you say that!'

'Do...do you forgive me for saying those awful things to you, darling? I didn't mean them, you know...'

Molly could not help but relent. 'Of course I forgive you,' she said gently. 'I love you, Mum.'

'Oh, Molly,' her mother cried, and threw her arms around her daughter.

Unfortunately, it was not the best time for Molly to be hugged. Her mother's display of affection tipped her over the edge on which she'd been balancing for several hours, splintering the brittle control with which she'd been holding in her misery. Her shoulders began to shake as sobs racked her whole body.

'Oh, Molly,' her mother groaned, and hugged her daughter even more tightly. 'Don't cry, darling. Please don't cry. Oh, you make me feel terrible. If only I hadn't said those awful things, you would probably have gone out with Liam when he asked you. It's all my fault!'

'No, it isn't,' Molly sniffled when she at last pulled out of her mother's arms. 'Liam only asked me out because Roxy's trying to prove some point or other and she's refused to have anything to do with him for a month. But come next Sunday they'll be back together again, as thick as thieves. Who knows? If she plays her cards right, he might even ask her to marry him.'

'What rubbish!' her mother pronounced firmly, startling Molly. 'Liam's not in love with that flashy bit of goods. No man in love with one girl looks at another girl as he looked at you today.'

Molly was dumbfounded. 'But I...I didn't notice him looking at me in any special way...'

'Then you're as blind as he is, my girl. You made a big mistake refusing to go out with him next Saturday night. Now listen here; when he comes over to pick up those papers, you tell him you've changed your mind and you'd like to go with him after all.'

'But...but...'

'No buts. You said he's not getting back with that Roxy till Sunday. Make the most of what time you have!'

'I was just going to say I don't have anything to wear,' Molly said, smiling weakly.

'Well, that's easily fixed.'

'How? Liam's accountant can't get us any more money immediately. And I'm not taking the cleaning money you earn, Mum. No way. One hundred dollars wouldn't be nearly enough anyway,' she added with a sad sigh. 'A dinner dress, complete with shoes and bag, doesn't come cheap these days.'

'Would five hundred dollars do?'

'Five hundred! But where...? I mean...'

Ruth smiled her pleasure at her daughter's surprise. 'You're not the only one who has rainy-day money stashed away, my girl. Come this way.'

Molly followed, fascinated, while her mother led her upstairs and into the master bedroom where she proceeded to lift up the mattress and draw out a battered brown paper envelope. She opened the flap and tipped the contents out onto the patchwork quilt. Notes of all sizes fluttered down, mostly fives, tens and twenties.

'I used to hide this in an empty washing powder box in the laundry when your father was alive. But now it's safe enough here. I know there's at least five hundred dollars, maybe more.' She gathered the notes up and pressed them into Molly's hands. 'I want you to buy yourself a dress which will knock Liam's eyes out!'

Molly hated the wild rush of elation which flooded her heart, for she feared she was setting herself up for a disaster of monumental proportions. No matter what her mother said and no matter what dress she bought, how could she seriously compete with Roxy? It was like comparing a nice little house wine with a top-brand French champagne. Roxy's extravagant self fizzed and sparkled. She was a special-occasion lady whereas *she*, Molly, was the common, everyday, value-for-money variety.

When Liam looked at her he only ever saw a familiar face. And everyone knew what familiarity bred. Contempt. Never chemistry.

Or was that how he'd seen her in the past? Dared she hope that her new look *had* evoked a new appreciation? Molly had told the truth when she'd said she hadn't noticed Liam looking at her differently today. But after his news about Roxy she'd been too upset to notice anything, and had avoided Liam's eyes as much as possible.

Could her mother's observations possibly be correct, or was she just trying to make her daughter feel better? She'd been very guilty over her earlier less than generous remarks.

Molly didn't want to get her hopes up too much.

And yet...

Something was stirring within her soul. Something she'd never felt before. Something rather wicked.

Roxy had called her a sly little piece. Maybe she was right, Molly thought with a steeling of her spirit.

Because I am not going to go quietly, Roxy, darling. Neither am I going to let you have Liam back without a fight. Come Saturday night, I'm going to use every female trick in the book.

The only trouble was...she hadn't read that particular book yet. She would have to depend on her feminine instinct.

The front doorbell ringing startled both of them.

'That'll be Liam,' Ruth said urgently. 'Now drop that money and go down and talk to him while I get those papers he wants. Tell him you've changed your mind about Saturday night, and ask him what time he wants you ready by. Be cool, though. Not overly eager.'

'Mum, you sneaky thing.'

'Well, there's no point in being easy. Any girl who looks as good as you do can play a little hard to get. Besides, men never want what they think they can have, gratis. They like a bit of a challenge.'

Molly went downstairs, shaking her head. Who would have believed that within her own shy reserved mother lurked the makings of a *femme fatale*? Heaven knew what would happen if the McCrae widow ever became a blonde!

Molly summoned up a pleasant smile to answer the door, resolving to watch this time for any sign that Liam looked at her differently in any way.

'Hello there again,' she said. 'Mum won't be a minute with those papers. Look, about next Saturday night, Liam. That was rude of me to dismiss your very nice invitation out of hand. I know what it's like to go to these things all alone…'

She didn't actually, because she'd never been to an awards dinner. But Molly had never lacked an imagination. Just think of all those times Liam had made love to her in her mind!

Unfortunately, she began thinking of one of those times right at this moment. It was her favourite scenario where Liam was concerned. He would bring her home to this door after a serious date and there would be much kissing and panting on the front porch. When she finally unlocked the door, he would push her inside, then scoop her up into his arms and carry her upstairs to her room where a three-foot bed was no barrier to true love.

Her mouth dried as she thought of their naked bodies blended tightly, writhing together. Her green eyes glittered as they began unconsciously to rove over the object of her desire.

Before they reached his waist, Molly swallowed then cleared her throat. 'Er...could I possibly change my mind and say yes?'

He stiffened. He actually stiffened.

Why?

'Is there a problem with that?' she asked airily, even while her heart was thudding.

He just stood there, frowning at her. The atmosphere on that doorstep was suddenly charged with a quite alien tension. Molly didn't know what to make of it except that she found herself holding her breath.

'Liam?' she choked out.

He seemed to have to shake himself to answer. 'No,' he muttered. 'No problem. I'll look forward to it.'

Molly had to be careful not to let all the breath out of her lungs in a rush. 'Fine,' she said with a small smile. 'Well, where is this dinner and what time should I be ready?'

'It's being held down at the League's Club, upstairs in the Admiral's Quarters. The dinner starts at eight.

Pre-dinner drinks at seven-thirty. I'll pick you up at...say...seven-fifteen?'

'I'll be ready. And thanks again for helping us with the finance business.'

'My pleasure.'

But it didn't look as if it was his pleasure. Not at all. He hadn't smiled once since she'd opened the door. Molly could not make head or tail of his mood, except that it was obvious he had mixed feelings about taking her to that dinner.

She prayed his reluctance was because he'd begun to feel things for her which he found confusing, and not because he was worried Roxy might get jealous, if she ever found out.

Her mother's arrival at that point steered the conversation to less stressful grounds. Liam left a couple of minutes later and as Ruth closed the front door she threw Molly a questioning glance. 'Well? What happened? You both seemed a little tense when I came down.'

Molly shrugged. 'I don't rightly know. I told him I'd changed my mind about the dinner, and he agreed to take me, but not with any great enthusiasm. To be honest, I think it worried the heck out of him.'

'Well, that's better than indifference, Molly.'

'That's what I was thinking.'

'Only time will tell, I guess.'

'I suppose so. But by golly it's going to be a very long week.'

CHAPTER EIGHT

'LONG' wasn't the word for it. 'Excruciating' was better.

Molly could not concentrate on her work. How could she, with Joan besieging her with suggestions from the moment she arrived at work on Monday morning and spied the newly made-over Molly?

Joan's main advice was directed at Molly's choice of clothing for the big night. The trouble was, she changed her mind every day. On Monday she insisted Molly buy black. Lace, preferably. Black lace was so-o-o sexy!

Molly didn't think she could carry off black lace and told Joan as much. So on Tuesday Joan moved to red satin…before she realised red would clash horribly with Molly's new hair colour. From Wednesday to Friday she went through every other colour in the rainbow, plus every possible style from strapless and sexy to tight and slinky, then finally to white and virginal.

This last, desperate idea was an attempt at reverse psychology, since Roxy would never dress in such a fashion.

Molly was glad to leave work on Friday afternoon, having informed her avid friend that she would simply buy something that suited and flattered her. Joan had pulled a face before pressing the solemn promise from Molly that she would finally wear the perfume she'd given her on her birthday.

'And buy yourself some drop earrings,' had been Joan's last hurrah. 'I was watching this body language expert on television the other day and he said dangling earrings projected highly sexual messages on some subtly primitive basis. It seems they bring attention to the earlobes, which was one of our earliest erogenous zones. Apparently there's this tribe in Africa where the women stretch their earlobes with heavy rings and weights. The ones with the longest earlobes are considered the sexiest, so the longer the earrings the better.'

Molly had sighed and agreed to wear long, dangling earrings as well as the perfume.

Saturday dawned slightly overcast but the sun came out during Molly's short train trip up to the shopping centre at Tuggerah. The forecast that morning had predicted twenty-eight degrees, average for the Central Coast in early March. Fortunately, the humidity was low so Molly would not have to worry about perspiration ruining whatever dress she bought.

She arrived just as the shops opened, her mother's gift of five hundred and forty-five dollars tucked safely in her purse. Four hours later her mission was finally accomplished, and her purse was pretty empty. Molly could hardly contain her excitement on the train ride home, hugging the parcels on her lap.

She would never have dreamt she could look so good. Or so sexy. Of course, it was to be seen what Liam would think of her, but she could never reproach herself for not pulling out all the stops.

She hurried home from the station, puffing a little as she struggled up the hill with her four plastic bags. It was just after one-thirty and Liam's red car was nowhere in sight. His mother was, though, Babs waving from where she was attending to her pot-plants on the front porch.

'Been shopping for tonight, dear?' she called out, her smile bright.

Molly was grateful to stop for a minute. 'Yes, Mrs Delaney. I've been very extravagant,' she confessed rather breathlessly. 'New dress. New shoes. New everything, actually.'

'Oh, you must come in and show me. I'd love to see them.'

Molly hesitated, then glanced back down the hill. She didn't want to be caught by Liam coming home. She didn't want him to see her today till she was ready.

'Don't worry,' Babs said. 'Liam's not due. He has to work all day today. He just rang to say he'd get ready down in Sydney and drive straight to your place. Come on. You can have a cool drink while you're at it. You look hot.'

Molly *was* hot. But it wasn't just from the shopping. Suddenly, tonight was all too real. It was also her last chance. If nothing came of tonight with Liam then she would have to give up all hope.

Total failure was less than a few hours away.

'What a lovely green!' Babs exclaimed when Molly drew the silk bit of nothing out of the bag. 'It reminds me of the colour of the water around the Great Barrier Reef. Hold it up against you,' she urged. 'Oh, yes, that's just the thing.' She chuckled delightedly. 'You're certainly going to make that boy of mine sit up and take notice in *that* dress, aren't you, my dear?'

Molly's eyes rounded at Liam's mother, who gave her a softly knowing smile in return. 'You think I haven't guessed all these years that you're in love with my son?'

'I... I...'

'You don't have to say a thing. Just listen. Liam does not love Roxy. She is, however, a beautiful and clever girl who panders to his not inconsiderable ego and knows exactly how to handle him.'

Molly was all ears as Liam's mother went on. She'd been riveted from the moment Babs had said Liam did not love Roxy.

'I know my son very well, Molly. I know his strengths and his weaknesses. Basically, he is a good, kind, loving boy, but he has an obsessive workaholic personality with a one-track mind. I'm sure you've seen evidence of this for yourself. I used to have to set an alarm clock next to his computer to get him to school reasonably on time. When he becomes absorbed in a project nothing can distract him, not even his male needs, which I might add are as strong as any other normal red-blooded man's.'

This wasn't any news to Molly. She'd seen the trail of girlfriends, all of them not exactly the types you just *talked* to on a date.

'You might think Liam has only ever been attracted to the most beautiful of girls,' his mother went on. 'That he's like a moth drawn only to the brightest of flames.'

'Well, his girlfriends have all been stunners, Mrs Delaney,' Molly pointed out.

'True. So I suppose if I said it was their personalities which won him you would be sceptical?'

Molly just laughed.

'I understand your cynicism. Nevertheless, what I am saying is true. The only girls who've attracted Liam have been the ones who had enough confidence in themselves to break through his absent-minded nature and force him to notice them. I have no doubt most of them approached him first, made none too subtle passes and flirted with him outrageously in order to win him away from his other, all-consuming passions.

'Naturally, the only girls who have such a degree of confidence are usually very beautiful ones which gives them that added edge. Once they have Liam's attention, they have the equipment to ensnare his sexual desire as well. Even so, he usually tires of them rather quickly. Either that or they themselves become frustrated with his tendency to forget dates, and they leave the relationship of their own accord.

'Roxy, however, has hung in there. I think she must be very good in bed. I also think she knows Liam's net worth and wants to hitch her wagon to a star. I suspect this so-called trial separation is supposed to frustrate Liam enough for him to agree to marry her. I don't know if it will work. I sincerely hope not, because she does not love my son and will make him miserable in the end. He does not believe in divorce, you see. Liam needs someone who truly loves and understands him. In short, Molly, he needs you.'

Molly was speechless.

'You have the perfect opportunity to put a spanner in Roxy's works tonight, my dear,' Babs continued in a conspiratorial voice. 'But you must be bold. And daring. Make him notice you, in more ways than one. Flirt with him. Let him know you want him. You *do* want him, don't you?'

All Molly could do was nod.

'Then go after him, with as much cunning and ruthlessness as Roxy did. In short, seduce him!'

Seduce him?

Molly went home with those daunting words ringing in her ears. How did an inexperienced virgin seduce a man like Liam? According to his own mother, he'd had countless sexy, beautiful women do just that and do it superbly! What chance did *she*, Molly McCrae, have? Made-over she might be, but that was only a skin-deep transformation. Inside, she was still a quiet, reserved kind of girl. Basically, she was not bold. Or daring.

Okay, so she'd spoken up for herself a few times recently, but only in private and with people she knew well. The thought of openly flirting with Liam in a very public place at a well-attended formal dinner sent frenetic butterflies fluttering around in her stomach.

Seven o'clock found those butterflies still in full flight. Yet her reflection in the dressing-table mirror went some way to boosting that confidence Liam's mother had insisted she find. Molly knew she had never looked better. Or sexier. Joan had certainly been right about those earrings. Outrageously long, the green crystal drops hung nearly to her shoulders, swaying seductively whenever she moved. They'd been worth every cent of the fifty dollars they'd cost.

'Oh, Molly, you look gorgeous!'

Molly swung round at her mother's voice, the A-line skirt of her green silk dress flaring out before settling into more discreet folds against her thighs. Not that a skirt that short could ever be really discreet. It ended a good five inches above her knees. When combined with the four-inch heels of her strappy, bronze-coloured Jane Debster shoes she looked all leg.

'Do you really think so, Mum?' Molly was desperate for reassurance, her own eyes not to be trusted.

Ruth's admiring gaze travelled from her daughter's shimmering hair, down over her perfectly made-up face, past the flamboyant earrings and finally to the very sexy little dress which showed off Molly's recently reshaped curves to perfection. The low, scooped neckline hinted at a very adequate and perfectly natural cleavage, the tight bodice and nipped-in waistline showing that Molly could rival Scarlett O'Hara in the hourglass figure department, and *without* the help of a corset.

'Turn around,' her mother said. 'Let me see the back again.'

Molly did so a little tentatively. She knew the lace-up back was daring, exposing a deep section of creamy flesh right down her back to her waist. This was part of the style of course, but it precluded the wearing of a bra, even a strapless one. The only underwear Molly had on, in fact, was an expensive pair of shiny skin-coloured Lycra tights which had built-in tummy-control panties.

Molly turned back to find her mother frowning slightly. 'What's wrong?' she asked, panicking. 'Do you think the neckline is too bare? Should I wear a necklace instead of these earrings?'

Ruth smiled reassuringly. 'Not at all. Those earrings are perfect. No, I was just hoping everything turns out right for you tonight.'

Molly scooped in a steadying breath. 'I do too...'

Ruth came forward to take her daughter's hands in hers. 'Whatever happens, you look lovely.'

'Thank you, Mum.'

'You smell lovely too. What's that perfume you're wearing?'

'It's the one Joan gave me for my birthday. It's called...Seductress.'

Ruth's eyebrows shot up. Mother and daughter looked at each other, then laughed.

'Let's hope it has a secret ingredient,' Molly said, shaking her head ruefully, 'because I think I'm going to need it.'

'You'll do fine, love. Just be your sweet lovely self and Liam will be enchanted.'

Now Molly felt confused. She had Liam's mother telling her to be a vamp, her own advising the natural approach. She had an awful feeling neither would work. The only time she'd had a real response from Liam was when he'd been jealous of Mr X.

Maybe that was the way to go. Mr X had been very useful so far...

Molly was speculating on how she could use Mr X to further advantage tonight when the doorbell rang. Her stomach immediately cramped. Oh, dear heaven.

'That will be Liam,' her mother whispered. 'I won't come to the door. Say I'm in the bath or something. If he has those papers for me, just put them on the hall table. Oh, and don't worry about how late you get home. *I* won't. In fact I won't worry too much if you don't come home at all!'

Molly's green eyes rounded at this amazingly broad-minded mother she'd suddenly acquired. 'Mum,' she said. 'I'm shocked. But I love you for being so understanding. Still, I think you'll find I'll be home soon after midnight like a good little Cinderella.'

'I don't know about that,' Ruth said wryly with another glance at her striking-looking daughter. 'Now off you go,' she added when the doorbell rang a second time.

Molly picked up the bronze clutch purse which matched her shoes and made her way carefully downstairs, taking her time lest she trip over in her new high heels.

Be confident, she kept telling herself as she approached the front door. And bold. And daring.

Schooling her face into a cool smile, she swung open the door, prepared to accept Liam's surprised admiration as though it were the most natural thing in the world. Unfortunately, she hadn't prepared herself for being confronted with Liam standing there looking blisteringly handsome in a superbly tailored black dinner suit.

Most men looked good when dressed in a tux.

Liam was breathtaking.

She stood there in speechless admiration of *his* beauty and missed his initial reaction to her own appearance. By the time she'd recovered sufficiently to look into his eyes he was shaking his head at her with a mildly rueful reproach.

'I can see this is going to be a long and difficult night.'

Molly was taken aback. Did he like the way she looked, or not? 'What do you mean?'

'You know very well what I mean, you minx. My God, are you wearing any underwear at *all* under that excuse for a dress?'

Molly blushed and bristled at the same time. 'I'm only following *your* suggestions. You told me you don't like women who wear pants.'

His shocked blue eyes zoomed to where the hem of her skirt ended at mid-thigh. Molly rolled her own eyes. 'That's not what I meant. I *do* have pantyhose on with built-in panties,' she said drily. 'I was talking about my wearing a dress and not a pants suit.'

'Oh, that's a dress you're almost wearing, is it? I though it was a left-over from a lingerie party.'

'Very funny. Truly, Liam, you're acting like some over-protective big brother, though I don't know why. You never have before.'

'You've never looked like *this* before.'

'It that a compliment or an insult?'

'It could be a damned problem.'

'I don't see how,' she said airily. But she wasn't as thick as she was making out, and the reality of Liam's brooding reactions thrilled her to bits. He was perturbed by how she looked. And already jealous of any other man she might attract tonight.

His own mother's words popped into her mind. 'Go after him, with as much cunning and ruthlessness as Roxy did...

'So,' Molly went on, twirling around and mercilessly pretending she had no idea of the effect the back of the dress would have on him. 'Will I knock 'em dead at the dinner?'

'I don't know about the others,' he growled, grabbing her wrist to stop her from twirling round again, 'but I'm in my grave already.'

She feigned a flustered frown. 'But I'm not talking about *you*, Liam. I was thinking of all those successful and possibly available businessmen at this dinner night.'

Liam glared at her. 'So that's why you changed your mind about partnering me tonight? Because you want to parade yourself for other men's eyes, like you're in some kind of meat market?'

'Well...I wouldn't put it quite so crudely. And I'm really only interested in *one* man's eyes.' Molly only meant she wasn't the sort of girl who played the field, but Liam immediately took it the wrong way.

'*One* man?' He frowned, then scowled. 'Oh, my God, don't tell me your infernal Mr X is going to be at this bloody dinner tonight!' he bit out.

Molly tried not to colour guiltily, but failed. For the first time, the use of Mr X had backfired on her.

'Damn and blast it, Molly!' Liam exploded. 'You should have told me.'

'Why? Would you have refused to take me if I'd said he was going to be there?' she asked, even while her mind raced. Mr X simply had to be disposed of once and for all, she decided. He'd been very useful up till now, but suddenly he was beginning to get in the way.

Liam opened his mouth to say something, then snapped it shut again.

'It's an irrelevant question anyway,' Molly went on swiftly. 'Because Mr X is *not* going to be there. Mr X has been wiped from the planet from this moment onwards. I've decided to take your advice, Liam, and move on. This is me moving on. Now, do you think *we* might move on and get going? Or do you want to be late and make a grand entrance?'

'With Moving-on-Molly by my side?' he mocked. 'Heck, no. I'd much prefer to slink in the back door.'

'There's no pleasing you tonight, is there?' she snapped as she stepped outside and banged the door shut behind her. 'I only did everything you told me to do. I happen to think I look very nice.'

Liam gripped her nearest elbow and began urging her along the front path. It set her crystal earrings swinging, along with her unfettered breasts. She kept her eyes straight ahead but had a feeling Liam was glaring daggers at her highly mobile bust. She hadn't realised till that moment what substantial movement did to braless breasts. Ones of her size, that was.

'"Nice" is a very ineffectual word to describe how you look tonight,' Liam muttered.

Molly extracted her arm from his grip once they reached the passenger door of his car. 'So how would *you* describe how I look?' she challenged.

His blue eyes blazed as he yanked open the door and waved her inside. Not a word passed his lips while she lowered herself into the seat, but his eyes spoke volumes when they dropped to take note of the way her skirt rode up dangerously high when she sat down.

'Provocative,' he snarled at last, then banged the door shut.

'Good,' she snapped back, once he'd settled himself behind the wheel. 'That's exactly the look I was looking for tonight.'

Molly dropped her purse into her lap, noting with some dismay that the smallish bag covered almost half of the minuscule skirt. Had she gone too far with the dress? She wanted to attract Liam, not revolt him. She'd had no idea he could be such a prude. He certainly wasn't around Roxy. Good God, some of the gear that girl wore was downright disgusting!

Still...at least she *did* have his attention. That was something.

Pulling the seat belt out, she was in the process of buckling herself into place when Liam's hand shot out and gripped her chin. She gasped when he wrenched her face round his way, then gasped again when his mouth was suddenly covering hers.

His lips pressed down hard, insistent in their demand for surrender. She yielded more from shock than any immediate passion. Her lips fell apart and his tongue plunged deep into her mouth.

Her whimpering moan seemed to snap him back to the reality of his quite savage kiss, for his head whipped back abruptly, his eyes widening. She just stared at him, the back of her left hand coming up to cover her still stunned mouth.

He groaned and shook his head, clearly appalled at himself. 'I'm sorry, Moll. Hell, I don't know what got into me.'

Molly didn't believe him. He knew darned well why he'd done what he'd done. But by adopting ignorance of his very male actions he was throwing the ball in her court. How she acted now would set the tone for the whole evening.

Her hand trembling slightly, she removed it from her mouth and reached out towards him, letting it come to a shaky rest against his cheek. She twisted and leant towards him till her mouth was only inches away from his. '*I'm* not,' she whispered, and made the momentous decision to close those inches.

His shock was even greater than hers had been. For a few excruciating moments his mouth froze under her kiss. Molly hesitated herself. Good God, if he wrenched his mouth away, what would she do? Impossible to laugh it off. She would be utterly crushed.

Don't be tentative, came the voice of desperation. Be bold! Be daring!

She lifted her mouth from his and smiled. 'What's the matter, Liam? Haven't you been kissed back by a girl before?'

He didn't say a word, just kept staring at her as if she were a stranger.

Sighing, she dropped her hand away from his face

and settled herself back in the passenger seat. If nothing else, she'd taken the initiative and salvaged her pride.

'It's not that,' he growled as he fired the engine. 'Let's be honest, Moll. It's not *me* you really want to be kissing anyway, is it? Look, I won't say you're not a temptation, looking as you look tonight. But might I also remind you that I'm supposed to be getting back with my girlfriend tomorrow? I don't like complications in my life, and if I don't watch myself you might become a complication. So let's just keep our old status quo going, if you don't mind. We're good friends. Nothing more. I'm sorry I kissed you just now. I promise you it won't happen again.'

Molly bit her bottom lip and turned her face away to stare through the passenger window. Her immediate response to Liam's words was to sink back into herself, and oblivion. Underneath, she'd expected failure, hadn't she? Game, set and match to Roxy!

But it seemed her new appearance had imbued her with more confidence in herself that she would ever have believed. Or maybe it was everyone else's confidence in her. Whatever, her mind gradually turned more positive, clinging to the fact that Liam hadn't mentioned Roxy as his first excuse for backing away. His initial withdrawal had been because he thought she didn't really want to be kissing *him*. He mistakenly thought he was just a substitute for Mr X.

Molly's frustration was acute. She heartily wished she'd never invented Liam's mysterious alter ego! She toyed with telling Liam the truth during the tensely silent drive down to Gosford. That *he* was Mr X, that she was crazy about him and would do anything for him.

But by the time Liam turned into the club car park ten short minutes later she'd abandoned that idea. It smacked too much of desperation and would send any man running in the opposite direction. No, her mission tonight was to seduce Liam, not openly declare her undying devotion.

Tomorrow was several hours away and she aimed to make the most of them.

Now, what had worked best for her this past week or so?

Jealousy.

But not over Mr X this time, she decided. Over some other man.   Molly hoped and prayed there would be a suitable candidate at this dinner tonight, and that he would find her as provocative as Liam had.

CHAPTER NINE

THE League's Club had been the main social hub of the Central Coast area for some years. Membership was cheap, and not even necessary to gain entrance. Visitors and tourists were welcome to enjoy the many facilities and entertainments the club had to offer. There were poker machines galore, bingo nights, discos, variety shows, bars, lounges, snooker tables and even a TAB betting branch. The large bistro section provided inexpensive meals, with three other restaurants catering for patrons who wanted a more extensive menu and silver service.

Then there were the large rooms on the first floor set aside for conferences, weddings and award dinners.

It was understandable, then, that the club car park was almost full by seven-thirty on that Saturday night. Liam finally found a spot on the top level, his face showing irritation by the time he and Molly made their way over towards the lifts. When a black Jag sped around the corner from the level below and almost collected them, Liam could no longer contain his temper.

He swore, shaking his fist at the unseen driver.

The Jag screeched to a halt. The tinted window

purred down and Dennis Taylor's distinctive dark head leant out.

'Liam!' he exclaimed. 'I thought it was you I nearly killed. Pretty stupid of me since I gather you're presenting me with my award tonight. I was voted Young Businessman of the Year, would you believe?'

Dennis's deeply set dark eyes suddenly shifted to Molly, his heavy black brows shooting upwards. 'Good God, is that our little Molly you've got with you? Wow, girl, you're looking even better than you did the other night. Hold the lift for me, you two, will you? It won't take me a sec to park this old chariot.'

Liam's grip on her arm tightened as he steered her over to the lift. '*Our* little Molly?' he grated out. 'What did he mean by that? And where in God's name did he see you the other night?'

Molly thought all her Christmases had come at once. She could not have orchestrated things better herself. Fate had, for once, been on her side.

'Dennis drove by as I was walking home from the hairdresser Friday week ago,' she said truthfully. 'He stopped and gave me a lift home.'

Liam reached out with his free hand and jabbed the 'down' button before glowering down at her. '*And?*'

Molly had no trouble adopting an innocent expression. She *was* innocent. 'And what?'

'And he told you you looked fantastic, didn't he?'

Molly stiffened. Suddenly, she could see which way Liam's mind was working and it wasn't what she wanted at all. Damn that infernal Mr X!

'He did say something complimentary,' she hedged. 'I can't really remember his exact words.'

'Don't play games with me, Moll. You're not likely to have forgotten the exact words your precious Mr X said to you. Dennis Taylor *is* your Mr X, isn't he? You lied to me about that. And you lied to me about knowing he'd be here tonight.'

'Don't be silly, Liam.' She shrugged out of his bruising hold. 'Dennis is *not* my Mr X and I had no idea he would be here tonight. But now that he is I can't say I'm sorry. I've always liked Dennis. He's good fun.'

The lift doors slid open and they walked in, Molly and not Liam reaching for the 'hold' button.

'You do realise that he'll try to hit on you,' Liam pointed out scathingly.

'Will he? Well, why should that worry you?'

'Your even saying that shows your naivety,' he snapped. 'God, you're a bloody babe in the woods where men like Dennis Taylor are concerned. I wouldn't trust him with an eighty-year-old grandmother, let alone a silly young thing like you who's set her sights on *moving on.*'

'I don't think Dennis is as bad as everyone makes him out to be,' she defended hotly, her face burning over Liam's calling her naive and silly.

'I wouldn't advise your putting that notion to the test,' he ground out.

An awkward silence fell between them, broken only when Dennis strode into the lift. He was wearing a dinner suit of similar ilk to Liam's, but somehow it just didn't look as good on him. Not as elegant. Or as impressive, in Molly's opinion. They said clothes maketh the man. In Liam's case it was the other way around.

'Thanks, babe,' Dennis said, pressing the ground-floor button while openly ogling Molly. 'So how come you two are out together tonight? Last time I saw you, Liam, you had a big blonde bombshell on your arm.'

'Liam and I are just good friends,' Molly piped up before Liam could say a word. 'His girlfriend couldn't make it so I'm here in her place.'

Dennis looked decidedly pleased at this news. 'So you're not on a real date?'

Molly laughed. 'Good heavens, no!'

'So what are you doing later, *after* the dinner?' he persisted.

Molly had to give Dennis his due. He didn't believe in wasting time.

'I'm taking her home,' Liam pronounced firmly.

'Come now, old chap, don't be a spoilsport,' Dennis said cajolingly. 'If you're not interested in this little lady, then I surely am.'

'Then I suggest you ask her out some other time,' Liam said politely, even though his eyes would have set low-calorie jelly in ten seconds flat. 'Contrary to Molly's opinion, I *do* consider this a real date. When I take a girl out for the night, I see her safely home.'

The subtle emphasis on the word 'safely' did not

escape Molly. Or Dennis, who rolled his eyes and snorted.

'I didn't realise you were so old-fashioned.'

'I don't consider myself old-fashioned. But I do have certain standards.'

Dennis guffawed. 'Yeah, I've seen some of them. And I must congratulate you on your standards. When you've finished with Blondie, you can give me her phone number.'

The lift doors opened, and Liam took Molly's arm. 'Find your own girlfriends,' he advised brusquely. 'And leave Molly alone.'

Dennis grinned. 'Them's fighting words, Liam.'

Molly was astonished by the look Liam sent Dennis. She'd always thought of Liam as a pacifist. Violence would never be his way. But there was violence in his eyes when he glared at his former classmate.

'Any time, Dennis,' he said in a voice reminiscent of Clint Eastwood at his tough-guy best. 'Anywhere.'

Doubt filled Dennis's face. He glanced from Liam to Molly to Liam again. In the end he shrugged and stalked off.

Molly couldn't make up her mind if she liked Liam's proprietorial manner or resented it. Whatever, her blood was up, and so was her temper.

'I don't understand your dog-in-the-manger attitude,' she hissed on their walk from the lift to the club entrance. 'You don't want me, but you don't want any other man to want me.'

'Who says I don't want you?' he hissed back.

Molly ground to a halt, her crystal earrings in pendulum mode as she gaped up at the man she loved. But his returning glance was rueful and not full of the out-of-control, smouldering passion she was hoping for.

'Any red-blooded man would have to be dead not to want you, the way you're looking tonight,' he ground out. 'You must have got some inkling of the effect you had on me when I kissed you earlier. I had to exercise considerable self-control to stop when I did.'

'No kidding,' Molly muttered. And she knew just how he'd found that self-control. He'd only had to think of Roxy tomorrow, she thought with savage despair. Why waste all that pent-up male sexuality on silly, naive, innocent Molly when you have a blonde sex-bomb just waiting in the wings?

Her green eyes flashed as they raked over his handsome face. 'Congratulations on your self-control,' she said caustically. 'But what good is that to me? I told you I wanted to move on, Liam.'

'Meaning what?'

Molly's laugh was dry. 'And you called *me* silly and naive. Do I have to spell it out for you? I'm sick and tired of waiting for the man I love to love me back. And I'm sick and tired of being a virgin. Everyone keeps telling me to move on, even you. Well, I've decided to do just that tonight in a way where there's no turning back. Since you won't oblige me, Liam, then I'll find someone who will.'

'You don't mean that, Molly,' he said in truly shocked tones.

'I do mean it.'

'Not Dennis, for pity's sake!'

'Why not Dennis? I'm not expecting him to love me. Just to *make* love to me! I hear he's pretty good at that.'

Liam groaned. 'I can't bear to think of it.'

I can't bear to think of you and Roxy tomorrow, Molly agonised. 'Well, you know what to do in that case,' she threw at him in one desperate, last-ditch attempt. 'Do the honours yourself. If you were really my best friend, you would.'

He just stared at her as though she were mad.

She whirled and began to stride on ahead, her skirt swishing angrily around her legs. She was mad all right, mad with herself. If she had any real guts she'd take Dennis up on his offer. Who knew? Maybe she would before the night was up.

Liam caught up with her just as she approached the floor-to-ceiling glass doors which led into the club's brightly lit foyer. His arm linked forcibly with hers, slowing her step before turning her to face him.

His blue eyes burned down at her with a darkly angry frustration.

'All right,' he bit out. 'I'll do it. But be it on your

head, Moll. God knows, I seem to have suddenly lost mine!' And, with that, he swing her round and swept her into the club.

CHAPTER TEN

MOLLY would be eternally grateful that other people pounced on Liam as soon as they entered the club, because she was in a state of shock. Good manners had her smiling and saying the right things on automatic pilot, but it was a real relief that she couldn't have a private conversation with Liam at that point. She needed time to assimilate what had just happened, what he'd just agreed to. She needed time to calm the panic within.

But time brought little calm, only the most debilitating cluster of nerves. Her mind whirled with a possibly inaccurate memory of a saying which was perversely apt for the occasion, and went something like this: Careful of what you might want, because one day you might get it.

Molly now appreciated that acting out a scenario in one's imagination—however endlessly—was no preparation for actually living it. One of her most persistent and dearest fantasies was going to come true tonight, and her only feeling was terror! Where was the heady excitement which permeated her dreams? Where was the wild elation? The ecstasy?

Nowhere in damned sight, that was where! In their place was a gut-twisting apprehension, a suffocating sense of disbelief and an overwhelming feeling of inadequacy.

Naturally, she could not eat any of the dinner placed in front of her. Not a bite. Liam, however, was not similarly stricken. He ate his food while chatting casually with the others seated at the official table, acting as if he had nothing untoward on *his* mind. Clearly, his agreeing to deflower his best friend after the dinner was over did not rate as a sufficient reason to go off his food. He might have lost his head but he hadn't lost his appetite!

Men, Molly decided with growing cynicism, were a different breed altogether. Their egos, never their feelings, dictated all their actions. Liam was only taking her to bed because he could not bear for Dennis to. It had nothing to do with desire for her and everything to do with male competitiveness.

She moved her food around the various plates, trying to make it look as if she'd eaten something. She found some comfort in continuously sipping her wine, an easy task since her glass was never empty. The very attentive waiter kept topping it up, perhaps because from his elevated position he could peer down her cleavage.

When he went to top it up again during dessert, Liam's hand suddenly appeared over the glass, barring the way. Not a word was spoken. But the waiter got the message. After he'd moved on to attend to others at the table, Liam leant towards her.

'Under the circumstances, a reasonable alcoholic

consumption could be beneficial,' he said quietly. 'Too much, however, would definitely be counter-productive.

'Unless, of course, you wish to be close to unconscious when I take you to bed,' he added on a dry note. 'I do realise I'm not your first choice for this honour, but I would like you to at least remember who was responsible the next morning.'

Molly felt totally miffed. So she'd been right! Liam's decision to be her first lover *was* just a matter of ego. She vowed to find something cutting to say in return, but floundered abysmally.

The Master of Ceremonies' introduction of the night's guest speaker put Molly out of her misery. Liam rose from his chair to walk up onto the stage which had been set up at one end of the long rectangular room, standing to one side of the podium while the MC ran through a praise-filled résumé of Liam's achievements in business. Molly wasn't really listening. She was too busy staring at Liam, at this absolutely gorgeous man whom she'd adored for years and who, in a couple of hours' time, would hopefully do what she'd always wanted him to do.

And she'd been stupidly sitting there, finding fault with him and indulging in all sorts of insecure female rubbish.

Good God, what was wrong with her? This was the stuff romantic dreams were made of. She'd accused Liam once of never stopping and smelling the flowers yet here she was, letting panic and pride spoil what should be the happiest night of her life.

Well, from this moment on tonight, she was going to stop and smell the flowers. She would not question Liam's motivations for making love to her. She would not worry about tomorrow. She would simply enjoy each moment for what it was and let the rest of the world go by.

Her eyes softened as they watched Liam step up to the podium, looking so sophisticated and impressive. With her silly anger gone, she listened to every word he said, quickly rapt in the power and sincerity of his speech. He spoke of achievement in terms of faith in one's own ability and that unswerving tunnel vision which refused to accept defeat and called every seeming failure a learning experience. He did not gloss over the necessity of hard work, nor the difficulties of the present economic climate. He was passionate and inspiring. You could have heard a pin drop in the room. Molly felt so proud.

That's the man I love, she wanted to call out to everyone.

But of course she did not. She sat there silently, vowing that tonight she would show Liam that love, in every touch, every caress. She might not have Roxy's expertise in bed, but she would give him something the other woman could not. True love. And true passion. Nothing feigned or faked.

When Liam finished his speech, the room erupted

with applause, Molly clapping as enthusiastically as everyone else.

After that, it was time to get on with the award-giving, Dennis coming lucky last. When he strode up onto the stage to accept the award, Molly tensed a little. But no one would have guessed the two men were anything but the best of friends, both of them smiling broadly while the photographer snapped them together.

But Dennis whispered something after the photographer had finished, something which had Liam frowning momentarily over at Molly. He said something back to Dennis, who made another remark then laughed and clapped Liam on the shoulder. By the time Liam sat back down next to Molly, she could not contain her curiosity.

'What did Dennis say to you just then?' she asked tautly.

'When?'

'Just then!' she repeated, frustrated.

'Dennis never says anything of importance.'

'But you frowned at me afterwards.'

'Did I?'

'You know you did.'

'It was nothing. Just Dennis being Dennis. He's always been a bad loser. Come on. Let's go.'

When he stood up abruptly, Molly gaped up at him. 'Now? You want to go *now*?'

'Yes. Why not? Surely you don't want to stay here and make meaningless chit-chat? It's already ten-thirty. It'll be nearly midnight by the time we make it to my place. If I'm to deliver you back home before the dawn I think we should shake a leg, don't you?'

'Well, I... I...' To tell him that her mother would not worry if she didn't make it home before the dawn would have been met with much scepticism. 'Fine,' she finally said, her voice not much more than a squeak.

Swallowing, she stood up and let Liam propel her shaky legs from the room, and the club.

'Where exactly *is* your place?' Molly queried on their way to the car. She knew if she didn't talk she would simply die of tension. 'I mean, I know you jog to your office in North Sydney every morning, but I'm not sure where you live.'

'My old place was in St Leonards, but I bought a new apartment in one of those new inner-city high-rises a couple of months back. I only moved in this last week, though.'

'A new car, and now a new place,' Molly remarked casually, though her heart was singing with the thought that if he'd only moved in this last week he'd never spent time alone with Roxy there, never slept with her in that particular bedroom. Who knew, maybe even the bed was a new one?

Thinking about bedrooms and beds brought a re-surgence of nerves which reminded her forcibly of her empty stomach. Maybe she should have tried to eat something. The last thing she wanted was her hunger pains making embarrassing noises when Liam made love to her.

They reached the car and Liam opened the passenger door for her. Their eyes met and Liam's were irritatingly unreadable. If he was nervous about the rest of the evening, he certainly wasn't showing it.

'You're not the only one who's decided to make changes in their life,' he said matter-of-factly. 'Turning thirty made me realise time was moving on.'

Oh, my God, she thought. He *is* thinking about marrying Roxy. 'Thirty's not that old, Liam,' she said hastily. 'I mean, not for a man. Now, it might be for a woman because she has to have the babies, but in a man's case there's no need for him to rush into marriage.'

'Marriage! I wasn't talking about marriage. I was talking about enjoying some of the money I've worked so hard to make. Oh, do just get in. And don't, for pity's sake, gabble at me all the way to Sydney. I like to listen to music when I drive. And I like to concentrate. That excuse for an expressway doesn't suffer fools behind the wheel.'

Liam slotted an Enya CD into the built-in player before easing out of his parking space. Maybe *he* found her music relaxing, but Molly discovered a disturbing eroticism in several of the numbers, especially the ones with a repetitive and very rhythmic beat.

The next hour seemed eternal. Molly stared through the passenger window, first into the blackness of the countryside, then later at the city lights. She tried every method known to mankind to still her churning stomach. Deep, even breathing. Meditation. More common-sense reasoning of the type she'd soothed herself with at the dinner.

This is what you've always wanted. Stop being such a silly ninny. Liam knows what he's doing. He's an experienced lover. It won't hurt. It's going to be wonderful. Simply wonderful!

These last thoughts had a small measure of success till they drew close to the Harbour Bridge, after which the butterflies in Molly's stomach reached plague proportions. When Liam slowed to join the toll queue on the other side of the bridge, creeping along at a snail's pace, her pressure-cooker tension simply had to find an outlet.

'You know you don't have to do this if you don't want to,' she blurted out.

His sideways glance carried total exasperation. 'If you think for one moment I'm going to let you back out now, then you have another think coming!'

'Yes, but if you don't really *want* to...'

'Don't *want* to?' he grated out. 'Are you mad? I'm sitting here in bloody agony, I want to so much. Hell, I've thought of nothing else all night!'

'Oh.' Molly was stunned, then thrilled by the dark frustration in his voice. She would certainly never have guessed by his manner. Maybe he wasn't doing this just because of ego after all. Maybe he really *wanted* her, Molly McCrae.

Or maybe any attractive female would have done

as well, came the added dampening thought. Clearly, he'd been celibate since his separation from Roxy started over four weeks ago. Maybe he was just dying for some sex, and she'd tipped him over the edge tonight with her provocative dress and flirty manner. Hadn't he said when he'd agreed to sleep with her that he'd lost his head?

'Look, just in case you're languishing under a misapprehension here,' Liam went on quite irritably, 'I am not sacrificing myself on the altar of friendship tonight. It's passion that sends men to bed with women, not compassion. I wanted you the moment I saw you tonight.'

Molly took little comfort from this confession. It sounded like a classic case of uncontrollable male frustration to her.

'So you can stop sitting there worrying I might stop this time,' Liam informed her with a savage sideways glance. 'My conscience is well and truly routed. And you can stop acting like a nervous bride on her wedding night. You knew exactly what you were doing tonight, you wicked little minx. I finally realised that. No one comes out on a date dressed like *that* without a preconceived game plan. You were determined to seduce some poor, unsuspecting male tonight no matter what, weren't you?'

'Something like that.'

It was finally their turn at the toll gate. Liam dropped the fee into the basket, then surged off as soon as the green light blinked on. They followed the

Cahill Expressway over the top of Circular Quay and around the back of the Domain where Liam turned right at a set of lights, heading back towards the city proper. Molly gasped when he did an abrupt left-hand turn, zooming across the pavement and down a dimly lit ramp into an underground car park. He braked hard at a barrier at the base where he leant out and used a plastic security card to gain entrance. Less than twenty seconds later he was easing his Mazda into the allotted parking space for unit 711.

Molly swallowed hard.

The curtain was about to go up on the biggest show of her life. For once, she was centre stage, the heroine of the play, with Liam her hero. Ten days ago this would have been unbelievable, unthinkable.

Yet here she was...

This is your one chance, Molly, a voice whispered in her head. Don't waste it.

I won't, she promised herself firmly.

Suddenly, the knots in her stomach began to unravel and a strange calm overtook her. Without waiting for Liam, she reached for the door handle and let herself out of the car. She felt oddly ethereal as she watched him climb out and walk round to join her. Almost as though she was having an out-of-body experience. She was here, yet she was also watching from afar.

'Are you all right, Moll?' Liam asked, frowning.

Her smile was dreamy. 'Yes. Fine.'

His frown deepened. 'You're not drunk, are you?'

'No. I don't think so.'

'You knocked back a lot of that wine over dinner. And you didn't eat much.'

'I didn't have much appetite,' she admitted. 'I was thinking of you, Liam. And of this.' Again without waiting for him she slid her arms around his neck, reached up on tiptoe and pressed herself against him.

He just stood there, deliciously acquiescent, while her lips found his in a series of light kisses which fluttered over his mouth like angels' wings. Molly was in seventh heaven, making soft, satisfied little noises in her throat. Her fingers stroked the back of his neck, her thumbs caressing the soft skin behind his ears.

Finally, Liam's lips parted and he sucked in a long, quivering breath. Molly's tongue immediately darted forward, connecting with his own tonguetip before it could retreat. She felt his hesitation, but ruthlessly ignored it, snaking her tongue deep into his mouth then winding it around the full length of his.

She was the original Eve, tempting Adam with the pleasures of the flesh, but combining her seduction with an even more subtle force. Her love for him. It gave her a power she could never have guessed at. And the will to exercise that power. She undulated her tongue—and her body—against his, and urged him on as females had been urging their menfolk since time immemorial.

His tortured groan startled her as his hands came up to grip her shoulders. His fingertips dug into her flesh and for a few moments his tongue took over and gave her a glimpse of how Liam might make love, once he really lost his head. Just as savagely he yanked her away from him, holding her at arm's length while he glared down at her with a blistering reproach in his blazing blue eyes.

'No, damn it,' he ground out. 'No!'

'But you said you wouldn't stop!' she cried in dismay.

'I'm not stopping, you little fool. I'm just changing the scene of the crime.' And, taking her hand, he began dragging her across the car park.

'The crime?' she echoed dazedly.

'Yeah. What you were doing to me just then was criminal. But don't you worry, Miss Moving On. I'll let you do whatever you fancy once we're in the privacy of my bedroom. In fact, I'll insist upon it!'

CHAPTER ELEVEN

LIAM'S apartment was on the seventh floor. It was expensive, spacious, modern. And practically empty.

'I have ordered furniture but it hasn't arrived yet,' he said as he ushered Molly across a huge expanse of pale blue carpet. 'But don't worry. I did manage to buy a bed before I moved in. I had them send one of the floor stock, complete with bedlinen.'

Molly's heart leapt. A brand-new bed, with virgin sheets, waiting for her and Liam. No bad vibes. No memories. No comparisons.

He led her into a huge master bedroom dominated by an equally huge bed with dark blue and maroon bedding. The large double-glazed window which stretched across behind it was covered with cream vertical blinds but no curtains. A door to the left led off to what she presumed was an *en-suite* bathroom.

'So what do you think?' he said as he shrugged out of his dinner jacket and reefed off his black bow-tie.

Molly tried not to stare when he began unbuttoning his shirt. She kept telling herself it wouldn't be the first time she'd seen Liam naked to the waist. He always mowed his mother's lawn like that in the summer. But this was different.

'I think we have all the essentials, under the circumstances,' she said, her crisp tone belying the thickening in her throat. 'A bed. A bathroom. And us.'

Liam laughed while he yanked the shirt-tails out from the waistband of his trousers. 'I don't know if I entirely approve of Moving-on Molly, but I won't deny you have me totally intrigued.'

'I would prefer turned on to intrigued,' she quipped, determined not to revert to the mouse she'd once been. Where had that got her? Certainly not into Liam's bedroom with Liam undressing in front of her!

'That goes without saying,' he said, and stripped off the shirt.

Molly swallowed. 'Does it? I've never turned you on before...' She locked eyes with his and by sheer force of will kept hers steady. She would not have been human if her earlier nerves hadn't returned—this was unknown territory, after all—but she was damned if she was going to show them.

'Shall I undress as well?' she asked, her hands going behind her back in search of the bow which anchored the laces. She could not find the ends and screwed her head round over her shoulder in a vain attempt to locate the wretched things.

Liam materialised behind her. 'Let me,' he said softly, and removed her shaking hands. 'I've been wanting to do this all night...'

Molly gasped when he bent to press tender lips to the nape of her neck, at the same time obviously pulling the right thread, for the restricting laces suddenly gave way. A tremor raced through her as he eased the narrow silk straps towards the edge of her shoulders, kissing her neck all the while. Another inch or two and the whole dress would fall from her body, slithering down to the floor to leave her near naked to his eyes, and to his touch.

Her heart turned over at the thought, then quickened. To have Liam touch her bare breasts…

His hands moved outwards and the dress slithered downwards. Molly gasped, then held her breath. It felt an eternity before his hands moved again. And when they did she moaned her frustration at his lack of speed.

They slid slowly up and down her goose-bumped arms before finally taking her arms and winding them around behind him.

'Yes,' he said thickly when she clasped them together at the back of his waist, effectively imprisoning herself against him. Her mouth dried at the feel of his bare chest pressing up against her own bare back. Her heart thudded heavily behind her ribs, her naked breasts jutting out impatiently for his touch. They seemed to swell with each passing moment, their eager tips stretching out and upwards in silent yearning.

Something else was swelling as well, making its presence felt against the cushioning curves of her bottom. Molly had never seen—let alone felt—an erect male before. She knew the theory, but somehow the reality felt different from her virginal imaginings.

Bigger. Harder. And with a mind of its own. Her own mind reeled at the inevitability of its final resting place tonight.

Dear God...

Liam's hands grazing down over her breasts brought her back to the present, thrusting any thought of pain to the back of her mind. Pleasure took its place—blissful, blinding pleasure. She gasped when his palms rolled over her nipples a second time, then groaned when he took each tender peak between his thumb and forefinger, playing with them till they burned and throbbed with the sweetest ache she had ever known.

But it wasn't only her breasts which burned and ached. Her whole body was swiftly becoming a furnace of frantic fire.

'Liam,' she whispered in pleading tones.

'Yes?'

'Please don't stop.'

'I won't,' he rasped, his mouth moving restlessly over her neck, kissing and sucking at her heated skin.

Molly shivered violently. 'I mean later. Don't stop. For anything.'

His hands froze on her breasts. His mouth lifted. 'Are you sure?'

'Yes.'

'What about pregnancy?'

Molly was taken aback. She'd actually been thinking of her pain stopping him. Now she realised what he was referring to, and shrank from the concept of him putting anything between them. She might only have this night with him and she wanted everything to be perfect.

'There's no danger of that tonight,' she reassured him hurriedly, desperate to have his hands and mouth back on her flesh once more. 'My period's due this week and I'm never late.'

'You haven't asked me if *I'm* any danger to *you*.'

Again that thought had not occurred to her. '*Are* you?' she asked, shaken.

'No.'

She shivered her relief. 'Then everything's all right, then.'

He spun her abruptly in his arms and cupped her face. 'Promise me you won't trust any other man like that,' he demanded. 'You've no idea the lies some creeps will tell not to use a condom.'

The realisation that he was already anticipating her sleeping with other men after him dismayed Molly. Silly, really. What had she expected? That he would discover how much he secretly loved her tonight and claim her as his and his alone for ever? What a romantic fool she was!

'Don't you worry about what I do with other men, Liam,' she said sharply.

'But I *do*. You're my friend and I care about you.'

'Really? You yourself said tonight this had nothing to do with friendship.' She stepped back and hastily stripped off her pantyhose and shoes, scooping the bundle of clothes to one side and straightening to stand naked in front of him. Her chin lifted defiantly, her green eyes glittering as she pulled the swinging earrings from her lobes one by one and tossed them on top of her green silk dress. 'You were quite right. This has *nothing* to do with friendship, Liam. Nothing at all!'

Too much passion in her voice, she realised.

But too late.

Liam frowned. Then frowned some more. 'And what has it to do with, Moll?' he asked slowly, his eyes searching hers all the while. 'I sure as hell hope Dennis wasn't right.'

'Dennis? What has Dennis got to do with this?'

'Nothing, obviously. But he seemed to think your feelings for me encompassed more than friendship. He said he was watching you while I made my speech tonight and he reckoned you were in love with me. He warned me not to tangle with your body since virgins in love were notoriously vulnerable. I didn't believe him at the time. I thought it was just Dennis making trouble. But now I'm beginning to wonder...'

Molly knew she had to act quickly or all would be lost. She hoped her laughter had just the right mixture of disbelief and dry amusement. 'In love with you? Oh, Liam, how very typically male! You and Dennis do have incredible egos, you know. In love with you, as well as my Mr X? I'm not that much of a masochist. But you *have* grown into a very attractive man, dear friend,' she said, undulating towards him with a sexy smile curving her mouth. 'And your experience with women is impressive. Why do you think I chose you for this exercise? No, Liam, I don't want your love tonight. I just want your body.' She pressed her palms against his naked chest and kissed the base of his throat, then slowly lifted her eyes back to his.

Was he angry with her? Or angry with himself?

Whatever, his blue eyes were blazing with something. He gripped her elbows and lifted her bodily off the carpet, carrying her over and tossing her back onto the bed. She lay sprawled there in a breathless silence, watching dry-mouthed as he proceeded to strip himself with rough, angry movements.

The sight of the unknown was as worrisome as she had feared. No doubt about it. This was going to hurt. She only hoped he remembered his promise not to stop. For anything!

CHAPTER TWELVE

LIAM joined her on the bed, scooping her up onto the pillows and taking her mouth in a savage kiss.

Molly didn't mind his anger. She welcomed it. Anger was much safer than far too accurate accusations. More kisses followed, not quite as savage, but definitely still on the merciless side, his tongue ravaging her mouth while his hands ravaged her body.

Molly was amazed at how arousing she found this less than gentle handling. She moaned when he kneaded her breasts, whimpered when he pinched her nipples. But they were moans and whimpers of pure pleasure. Yet nothing compared with the electric sensations his fingers evoked when they slid between her legs. Everything inside her leapt, then twisted tight. She gasped into his mouth, then held her breath.

But not for long. Soon she was whimpering beneath the twin onslaughts of his mouth and those knowing fingers. He seemed to know exactly where to touch her down there, teasing and arousing her till she was melting and burning for him. The blood pounded in her temples and her head swam. She felt as if she was going to burst.

Soon, Molly began to fear her body was heading for that explosive release which was much sought after, but which usually heralded a swift end to desire. She didn't want these delicious feelings to end. She wanted them to go on and on and on!

Liam seemed to know, however, just when to stop that particular activity, leaving her in a fever pitch of arousal. She was more than ready for him to stroke open the lips which guarded her virgin flesh, more than ready for him to slip his finger inside.

When that finger started sliding in and out, her flesh gripped him avidly, her low groans betraying her increasing frustration. She sucked frantically on his tongue. Her hips writhed on the bed. One finger eventually became two, then three, stroking her inner walls, making them swollen and slick with wanting.

Oh, God, the wanting. She had never felt anything like it; had never imagined, even in her wildest fantasy, that it could be like this. The twisting tension within her mounted, and gathered. If she didn't have him inside her soon, she would go mad.

One hand searched blindly for him; found him; caressed him. Her legs fell apart and her other hand came round to grip his bare buttocks and urge him to roll between her legs. His mouth burst from hers, his invading hand withdrawing to brush both of hers away. And then he was there, probing, taking her breath away.

It wasn't painful. But neither was it as pleasurable as she'd been anticipating. The feeling of pressure was intense, and almost uncomfortable. She could not help tensing and when he pushed a little harder she gave a muffled cry. Now there was real pain. Surely she must split open.

'Are you all right?' he asked, his hands cradling her face as he looked deep into her eyes.

'Yes,' she bit out. 'Don't stop.'

'But I'm hurting you.'

She clenched her teeth even harder. 'It doesn't matter.'

'Of course it matters!' And he withdrew.

She clutched at his shoulders in a panic. 'You promised you wouldn't stop,' she reminded him. 'You promised!'

'For God's sake, do you think *I want* to stop?'

The tears came then, and he cuddled her to him. 'Don't cry, Moll. Please don't cry.'

'But you mustn't stop,' she sobbed against his shoulder. 'You don't understand. You mustn't.'

'Hush, my sweet,' he crooned. 'Hush. I'm not really stopping. But you need to relax. We'll just talk for a while.'

'Talk?' she echoed, dashing the tears from her cheeks. 'What…what about?'

His smile was wry. 'How about my latest project? That's what I usually talk to you about.'

'There's nothing usual about this situation, Liam,' she said tautly.

'No,' he agreed slowly. 'No, there certainly isn't.'

Still, he did just that, nestling between Molly's legs while he explained his idea for his next computer game, to be accompanied by an original soundtrack.

As usual it was a brilliant idea which would amuse as well as entertain. Slowly, she did relax and was actually laughing at something he said when Liam made his move, penetrating her fully before she could do more than gasp in astonishment.

She stared up at him, eyes and mouth wide with wonderment. For there had been no pain. None at all!

'See?' he said. 'It was just a matter of relaxing.'

'Yes,' came her choked-out reply. The realisation that Liam was deep inside her, that they were one, that they were truly lovers now, was almost too much for her. She could feel her eyes pricking with tears. Her heart contracted, and so did her insides.

'Mmm,' Liam murmured appreciatively. 'That felt good. Do it again.'

'Do what?' she asked breathlessly.

'Squeeze me. With your insides.'

She did and Liam moaned softly.

'Don't stop,' he rasped.

She didn't, and soon he was surging into her body in time with her contractions, thrusting deep as she squeezed tight, then rocking backwards on her release. Any thought of tears was soon forgotten. Everything was forgotten except what she was doing, and what she was feeling.

Was it pleasurable?

Molly wasn't sure. But she could not have stopped for anything. Driven by a dizzying and compelling desire, she clung and clutched at Liam's bare back and buttocks, pulling him down onto and into her body, striving for an even deeper possession. He seemed of a similar state of mind, for he scooped his hands up under her buttocks and held her off the bed so that he could pump even more powerfully into her.

'God, Molly,' he muttered thickly. 'It's too much. I'm going to come. I can't stop it. I'm sorry...'

She wasn't. For so was she. She could feel it. And just as he exploded within her her own climax arrived, shocking her with its electric intensity, making her back arch and her lips fall apart as she gasped her ecstasy. Her spasming muscles gripped Liam's flesh with a fierceness which had him crying out loud. They shuddered together, moaned together, grew silent together as the spasming waves slowly subsided.

Liam eventually rolled over, but he did not withdraw. He took her with him, his hands stroking gently up and down her spine while she melted against his body.

Molly thought she had never felt anything as loving as those hands. She sighed a deep, shuddering sigh, then just lay there, savouring every precious moment, both of the present and the recent past.

Making love with Liam had been everything—and more than—she'd hoped for.

There again, she'd known she could not ever be really disappointed, no matter what. Even if she had not come, she would still have been satisfied, deep down in her heart. But she had to admit that finding such wondrous physical satisfaction had been an added bonus. If nothing else, she had experienced the ultimate with the man she loved. She only hoped Liam had enjoyed it as much as she had. He *seemed* to have done. But of course she had no way of knowing. Maybe he *always* came like that. Maybe what had been so special for her had been commonplace for him.

Suddenly, he sighed, his chest rising and falling beneath her. She turned her face and kissed him just above the heart, then laid her cheek against the spot. She could hear it beating strongly. Dear Liam. He had a good heart.

Molly yawned as the world started to slip away. Those hands kept stroking her and soon a blissful blackness claimed her mind—and her body.

She woke to find Liam shaking her shoulder and telling her it was time he took her home. He was dressed in his dinner suit once more, but without the tie. Her clothes, she saw, were laid out neatly for her on the foot of the bed.

'I'll be out in the kitchen,' he said brusquely. 'Don't be too long. It's after two already.'

Molly's heart sank as she watched him retreat from the room. She'd known Liam long enough to know when something was bothering him. He would go all quiet and brooding, a faint frown forming a permanent V between his brows as if he had a headache.

Did he now regret doing what he'd done? Was his conscience bothering him?

Perhaps he was worried about how this would affect their friendship. Or his relationship with Roxy.

Molly bit her bottom lip. Surely he wasn't going to *tell* her? There was really no need.

'Are you up yet?' Liam called out somewhat impatiently. 'I can't hear any movement in there.'

'Yes, I'm up.'

Molly scooped up her clothes and dashed into the bathroom, where, after a quick visit to the loo, she struggled into her pantyhose and dress. The big bathroom mirror showed a pretty ravaged sight. Her hair was all over the place and her lips looked bruised and swollen. With her purse left in the car she had no make-up or comb for repairs. She lifted her arms to finger-comb her hair back into place, the action making her aware of very tender nipples under her dress. Yet, surprisingly, she wasn't at all sore elsewhere. Maybe that would come later.

Finally, she replaced her earrings and slipped her feet back into her shoes. Pasting a smile on her face, she sallied forth from the room, determined to put Liam's conscience to rest.

He was standing at the counter of the sleek grey and white kitchen, sipping a mug of coffee, that troubled V firmly in place between his eyebrows.

'I'm ready,' she said breezily.

He lowered the mug and glared at her.

Molly was quickly unnerved. 'What's wrong?'

He shook his head, his face reproachful. 'You slay me, Moll. Anyone would think nothing had changed between us.'

'Nothing has. Or are you saying you don't want us to be friends any more?'

'I'm not sure what I'm saying!' he snapped irritably. 'All I know is I'm going to find it hard to forget what we shared just now. I hadn't realised how much I might enjoy making love with you. It has... complicated things.'

Molly could not believe it! He was upset because he had *enjoyed* her. He was thinking of breaking up their friendship because she now represented a temptation, a complication! She had never felt so hurt—or as angry—as she did at that moment.

'And you don't like complications in your life, do you?' she said caustically. What about *my* life? she was thinking. Why don't you give *that* a thought? I don't exactly do what I just did every night of the week, you know!

'No,' he replied slowly. 'I don't like complications.'

'Tough. Life is a bitch, Liam.'

'I don't know about life,' he growled, 'but I know a certain girl who's in danger of becoming one.'

'Then at least I won't be the odd one out with all the other bitches you've bonked!'

He slammed the mug down onto the benchtop, spilling coffee all over the grey granite surface. 'Don't you dare talk like that!'

'I'll dare whatever I like, thank you very much. You can't dictate to me! Who do you think you are, Liam Delaney? You're not my father, brother or boyfriend. You're not even my friend any more from what I can see!'

'And you're no longer the Molly I knew and loved. You've turned into a bloody monster. A sarcastic, stroppy, sex-mad monster!'

'Really! Sex-mad, am I? Well, I didn't see you knocking me back last night, Mr Perfect. Yet you're supposed to be getting back with sexy Roxy today, who I'm sure would have given you all the bonking you wanted. But you couldn't wait a few miserable hours to get a bit, could you? Not after doing without for four whole weeks! Yet *I* hadn't had the pleasure for twenty-five rotten years. But never you fear. I'm going to make up for lost time now. Just you watch me! Now I'd like to go home, please. Oh, and don't talk to me during the drive, thank you very much. I'm not in the mood for meaningless chit-chat with selfish, narrow-minded hypocrites!'

CHAPTER THIRTEEN

'So HOW did last night go?' her mother asked when Molly struggled out of bed shortly before midday. 'You must have got home pretty late. I was still up reading at one-thirty.'

Molly knew she could not bear a full confession at that moment. She was still coming to terms with the end of her relationship with Liam. In the cold light of morning, it was a bitter pill to swallow that she'd exchanged a lifetime of friendship for one night of fantasy.

Liam had delivered her home around three-thirty, neither of them having said a word to each other on the trip. When he'd tried to say something in the driveway she'd stopped him with a look and quickly alighted. In her room, she'd felt too shattered to cry. She'd undressed and climbed into bed and just lain there, staring up at the ceiling, trying to make sense of the whole man/woman thing. No clear answers had come to comfort her.

She'd finally dropped off around dawn, and had one of those awful dreams where she was travelling on a train and had lost her luggage. It was a frustrating dream which she had from time to time. Inevitably, she woke feeling dreadful. Not that she needed an extra reason that morning.

Liam didn't like her any more. She'd become a sex-mad monster in his opinion; a…complication. Molly knew he would not come around any more. And pride would stop her seeking *him* out. Their friendship was over, ruined by her love for him.

'Molly?' her mother probed gently.

She shook her head, unable to say anything.

Ruth sighed. 'I presume it didn't work out like you hoped.'

'No,' Molly managed.

'I see. I'm so sorry, love. I know how much Liam means to you.'

'*Meant,*' Molly said with a sudden and unexpected determination. She stood up from where she'd been drooping over the kitchen table, her shoulders slumped in defeat. Now they straightened, her chin lifting in defiance of her depression. 'Liam is the past, Mum. Today is the first day of the rest of my life, and I don't aim to waste it moping around. I'm going out.'

'Out? Where, out?'

'I have no idea. Yet. I'll think about it while I have a bubble bath.'

'A bubble bath? In the middle of the day?'

'Why not? Do you realise I still haven't used the bottle of bubble bath Joan gave me for Christmas? I think it's way overdue.'

'What…what about the papers?'

'Papers?'

'The financial forms Liam was going to leave with me last night. He must have forgotten them. Did he mention anything to you about them?'

'No, he didn't. But I'm sure he hasn't forgotten, Mum. Liam's not like that.'

'Do you think I should go over and ask him about them? He must be there. His car's in the drive.'

Molly flinched. The thought that Liam was physically so close rattled her momentary resolve to get on with her life. How could she go on, having won him in a fashion for one short night, only to lose him for ever?

'Yes, I think that would be a good idea,' she said briskly. 'He's probably still asleep but I'm sure Mrs Delaney will be up.'

Molly turned and fled the room before she weakened in front of her mother. Stay strong, she kept telling herself on her way upstairs. You must stay strong!

One hour later she was bathed and dressed in blue jeans and her new lime T-shirt. Her hair was still a little damp but swinging nicely around her perfectly made-up face. She'd also hunted out some large round gold earrings she'd only worn once, but which now really suited her new look and new hair colour. She'd thought about putting on the new gold chain necklace Liam had given her, but didn't want the constant reminder of him, so it stayed at the back of her top drawer. She did, however, spray a whiff of Seductress behind her ears.

No one would have guessed just looking at her that inside she was having the mental and emotional battle of her life. It would be so easy to give in and give up, to sink back into the miserable mousy nothing she'd once been. But to do that would be to waste all the changes she'd made. If nothing else she would remain grateful to Liam for being the impetus behind her making those changes.

Neither would she ever regret losing her virginity to him. How could she? She loved him. It angered her, however, that Liam had never recognised her love for him, when everyone else had, even Dennis. It had been easier for him to believe she'd suddenly turned into a sex-mad monster than to face the fact that there could be something else behind her choosing him to become her first lover.

'Molly?' her mother called out from downstairs, and Molly immediately tensed. She recognised that slightly sheepish tone in her mother's voice.

'Yes?' she called back curtly.

'Um…Liam's here. He wants to talk to you.'

Molly squeezed her eyes shut. Oh, God, why couldn't Liam have left well enough alone? It was finished. *They* were finished. She'd risked the substance for the shadow and she'd lost. She understood that. Why didn't he?

It looked as if she would have to spell it out for him again, because no way was she going to let him play with her emotions any more, no matter how innocent his intentions. The way to hell was paved with good intentions. Maybe she should remind him of that.

'I'll be right down,' she said stiffly. Gathering herself, she slipped her bare feet into her brown sandals and forced herself to go down and face Liam. Her mother passed her on the stairs, obviously deciding to make herself scarce.

Liam was in the kitchen, standing with his back to the sink, his arms crossed.

'You look awful,' she said.

He didn't, actually. He looked fantastic, even with dark rings under his eyes and his clothing not up to his usual sartorial splendour. He too was wearing jeans. Grey. Stonewashed. But his white T-shirt was crumpled and there wasn't a jacket in sight.

'You don't,' he returned, blue eyes washing over her. 'You look great.'

Molly declined to make a comment on that comment. 'What is it you wanted, Liam?' she asked coolly.

'Your mother says you're going out.'

'That's right.'

'Where?'

'That's none of your business.'

'I'm making it my business. Where are you going?'

She shrugged. 'I'm not sure yet. Anywhere.'

'In that case you can come anywhere with me.'

'Can I, now?'

'Yes.'

'Why should I?'

'Because I'm asking you to.'

'Not good enough.'

'It was…once. You used to be happy to go along with anything I suggested.'

Her smile was not very nice. 'Times have changed, haven't they?'

'Yes. And so have you,' he bit out.

Molly raised her eyebrows. 'Do I detect a note of disapproval there? I must admit I'm at a loss. Because I actually *did* do everything you suggested. This is your creation, Liam,' she said, uncrossing her arms and sweeping them down over her body. 'You made me what I am today. You even gave me a splendid initiation into the pleasures of the flesh. I will be eternally grateful. They say a lot of girls' first experiences aren't anything to write home about. I don't know about you, but I found mine fantastic. If nothing else, I will be eternally grateful to you for that.'

'I don't want your bloody gratitude.'

'Oh? What is it you want, then?'

'You.'

There was no denying the dark intent in his smouldering blue eyes. They raked over her, showing her with more than words what he wanted. Not love. God, no. There was nothing of love in the way he was looking at her. Lust, hot and strong, burned across the distance between them, branding her with its stunning heat. Molly's surface coolness vanished momentarily, swamped by a white-hot deluge of answering desire.

'Don't tell me it's not mutual,' he ground out. 'I can see the truth in your face. You want me as much as I want you, Molly. As complicated as this might get, once was simply not enough.'

She wasn't going to deny it. Impossible. Her heart was off and running, and so was her conscience. If I can't have his love, she reasoned recklessly, then I'll settle for his lust. I'll settle for damned well anything at this moment.

This realisation made a mockery of her earlier vow to get on with her life without Liam. She was condemned to always being weak where he was concerned. Love made a woman weak, she accepted. It was a sobering thought.

'What about Roxy?' she asked, proud of herself that she didn't sound as shaken as she was.

'You let me worry about Roxy.' He held out his hand and waited. She knew that to place her hand in his was to surrender to his wishes without reserve. From what she could see, he wasn't offering her anything but sex. He hadn't even promised to get rid of his old girlfriend.

Molly knew she could not cope with that. 'I won't share you, Liam.'

'I won't share you, either.'

'You won't go back to her?'

'Not if you come with me right now.'

And give me what I want...

These unspoken words haunted Molly, for she found them both dismaying and wildly exciting. It wasn't exactly what *she* wanted. Still, becoming Liam's bedmate was a temptation beyond bearing. She hadn't yet had her fill of him in a sexual sense, either, had she? Difficult to knock back such a chance. Impossible, really.

His face held a blackly triumphant satisfaction when she placed her trembling hand in his. His fingers closed tightly around its slender width and he yanked her towards him. Her lips parted on a breathless gasp as their bodies collided.

'So you're my creation, are you?' he murmured in a low, dangerously menacing voice. 'In that case I've created a monster. A manipulative, demanding, conscienceless monster.' He began stroking her neck, making her quiver with arousal and expectation. His eyes dropped to her mouth and she could feel the heat of his desire in their blistering blue depths. Any moment he was going to kiss her. She wanted him to kiss her, ached for him to kiss her.

'No, I'm not going to kiss you,' he ground out, his fingers stilling on her throat. 'Even though you want me to. You're going to learn to wait. You're going to learn a lot of things before I'm finished with you. You think you can play with people? You think you can use me then just move on to other men, other lovers?'

His fingertips pressed into the soft skin of her throat. 'Think again, my darling,' he snapped, blue eyes gleaming. 'Last night was only the first of many nights. And all of them will be with me. No one else. Not Dennis or even your pathetic Mr X. Soon, your lovely little body will only respond to me because I aim to make enslaving it to my will my next project.'

He laughed. It was definitely a Mr Hyde laugh. It sent shivers down Molly's spine.

'You, better than anyone, know how obsessive I can get about my projects,' he went on in a fearsome fashion. 'Nothing sways me from my goal. I promise you I will devote every minute of every day to the task, all my intellect, and every ounce of my energy. I will become your tutor, your master, your own personal devil, taking you to levels of surrender undreamt of even in your darkest, most decadent fantasy! You want sexual experiences? My God, I'll give you all you damned well want. And more!'

Molly gaped up at him, her eyes round, her heart pounding. This was a Liam she'd never met before. A madly impassioned, out-of-control Liam whose dark side had him firmly in its grip. But oh, my, the insidious attraction of that dark side. What would it be like to be the object of such a wild, ruthless obsession, to become his next project? Molly knew you wouldn't need much incentive to surrender to his sexual will. His impassioned words were already sending her on the path to that particular hell.

And hell it would eventually be. For she knew Liam well enough to know that his obsessions always burnt out. Once a project was mastered, he quickly lost interest and abandoned it, moving on to the next project. And then the next.

'So what have you got to say to that?' he snarled.

Molly decided enough was enough. She might be dying to volunteer as his next project, but she would not be bullied, or abused.

'My goodness, you must be in even more desperate need of some sex today than you were last night,' she replied airily. 'Why didn't you just say so instead of going on with all that macho rubbish? So I say... Lead on, Macduff. I'm with you all the way.' And, without waiting for him to explode, she brushed past his temporarily stunned self and dashed upstairs. 'Mum!' she called out. 'Oh, Mum! Where are you? Liam and I are going out for the day and we might be late home, so don't cook dinner for me...'

CHAPTER FOURTEEN

ANOTHER talkless drive to Sydney. More nerve-racking tension.

And doubts. Terrible doubts.

What am I doing? Molly agonised. This isn't me. I'm *not* a sex-mad monster. I know I'm not. So what am I doing letting Liam reduce me to nothing but a sexual challenge?

Celine Dion was belting out a song, singing about love in her distinctive style.

Love! God, but she was beginning to hate that word. And the state. Being in love was totally self-destructive. Look what it had done to her mother. She'd loved her father who'd been a rotter and a wastrel. He'd brought her nothing but heartache and misery.

Now here *she* was, her mother's daughter, wasting her love on the wrong man. Maybe Liam wasn't a rotter or a wastrel but he had one major flaw. He didn't love her back. If he did, he wouldn't be doing this, would he? He'd be...

Molly sucked in a startled breath as a possible defect in her reasoning broke through her mental ramblings. The question she'd just asked herself could have been the wrong question. What if she'd asked how Liam would be acting if he definitely *didn't* love her? If he disliked and disapproved of her new self as much as he said he did.

For one thing he would not have come over today. He would have been only too happy to see the back of her. He certainly would not have raged at her then vowed to turn her into some kind of sex slave!

Molly took a deep breath and tried not to get too carried away with this new theory to explain Liam's somewhat alien actions. It was always possible that she'd somehow captured his sexual interest in a way previously unknown to him, and he just could not handle his new feelings towards her. Clearly he was jealous of the idea of her with any other man. Could that be the result of his having been her first lover? Maybe he'd never deflowered a virgin before. Maybe it had evoked a possessiveness over her body which his male ego interpreted as sole ownership. A bit like the little boy who could not bear to share his toys.

Their arrival at Liam's place brought a swift end to this new and rather exciting train of thought. Still, Molly vowed to stop being so obsessed with her own feelings and more observant about Liam's. She appreciated, however, that cool reasoning was difficult when your nerve-endings were dancing and all you could think about suddenly was what Liam would do when they were alone in his apartment.

He seemed a little tense himself, dropping his keys at the door then fumbling with the lock. He finally flung the door open and stalked inside. Molly let out her long-held breath then followed in his wake. She was about to say something when a voice interrupted her, a low, husky female voice.

'Glad to see you finally came home, darling. I don't know about you, but this last month has been the longest in my life. So I didn't want to waste any time...'

Molly could not see who it was who had spoken. Liam stood in her line of sight. But she recognised the voice. Roxy had a very distinctive delivery.

'For pity's sake, Roxy!' Liam exclaimed. 'I have someone with me.'

Molly stepped out from behind Liam's suddenly frozen stance to see what had shocked him. Roxy was draped in the bedroom doorway, stark naked.

If ever Molly had cause to feel inadequate, it was at that moment. She could not fault Roxy's tall, voluptuous body. Anywhere. The only remote flaw she could find was that Roxy's nakedness confirmed what a jealous Molly had always suspected—that Roxy was not a natural blonde.

Still, such a small imperfection was little comfort in the face of such an amazing figure.

Roxy was only slightly thrown by the unexpected presence of another woman. Her artfully raised arms dropped languidly to her sides and she rolled her eyes at Liam in mild exasperation. 'Really, darling. This *is* the day we agreed to get together again. Had you forgotten? Maybe I left you alone for too long...'

She actually sashayed into the room, utterly unabashed at her nudity. Her long blonde hair shifted in sensual disarray across her shoulders, her melon-like breasts undulating sensuously, bringing attention to their lush size, plus their very pink, very pointed nipples.

Molly would not have put it past her to have painted the damned things, then iced them to their present stunningly erect state.

'Why don't you tell this little sweetie to run along?' Roxy said, waving a dismissive hand in Molly's direction. 'You really don't want to stay, do you, sweetie? Liam has clearly been a naughty boy in not telling you he already has a girlfriend.'

Liam glared his fury at her while Molly gathered all her courage. 'Actually, my name is Molly, not sweetie,' she said coolly. 'And I'm afraid it's *you* who's going to be leaving, Roxy, dear. Liam has indeed been naughty, but only in not calling you today and telling you it's over between you two. He's decided to move on, haven't you, *darling*?' And she linked arms with Liam, fluttering her eyelashes up at him as she gazed adoringly into his stunned face.

Roxy at last looked annoyed. Her hands found her hips and she peered at Molly with narrowed eyes. 'Molly, did you say?'

She took an aggressive step forward and looked Molly up and down. 'My God, it *is*!' she sneered. 'It's the mouse from next door. I just didn't recognise her. I always knew you were a sly little piece. Did you think you had me fooled with your butter-wouldn'tmelt-in-your-mouth routine? I saw the way you drooled over Liam when he wasn't watching. I knew you were jealous as sin of me and you were just watching and waiting for your chance to get your hooks in. Just good friends, my foot. That's not what you wanted. Never was!

'So what did she do to get you, darling?' she directed up at Liam. 'Confessed her long-time love? Kissed your feet? Promised undying devotion? No, I don't think that would have worked if I know you. You would have run a mile. You like your women assertive and independent, not simpering and clinging.'

She gave Molly another savage glance, then laughed. 'I get it. She played the make-over game. Changed her hair and clothes. Worked on her previously pathetic body, then threw you the oldest line in the book. Said she was off to spread her wings.'

'That's enough!' Liam ground out.

'Oh, no, it's not,' Roxy returned, scornful and defiant. 'It's not nearly enough. I'm going to have my say. I'm not going to crawl out of here with my tail between my legs. If nothing else I'm going to make you see that that bitch there is even more of a schemer than I am. And that's saying something, lover.

'So what carrot did you dangle for him, princess? Your priceless virginity?' When Molly's face flamed, Roxy sniggered. 'Oh, that *is* priceless. And you fell for it, Liam? I'm surprised. I thought you had more sophistication than that. But I guess deep down all men are suckers for supposedly untouched flesh, the poor misera—'

Roxy never got to finish her tirade of insults. She was too busy squawking when Liam threw her over his shoulder and marched her to the door. But she soon found her voice again, screaming a string of obscenities at Liam when he dumped her, in a none too flattering heap, in the hallway. Her clothes followed, then her purse—minus a key, an open-mouthed Molly noticed.

'Goodbye, Roxy,' he said coldly. 'I would have liked to have done this decently. But decency would be wasted on you. I'm sure you won't have any trouble finding some sucker who has the same low standards as yourself. And as filthy a tongue. *Hasta la vista*, baby.' And he slammed the door shut on her, shooting the lock across with a savage flick of his wrist.

When he turned, he actually shuddered. 'I can't believe I ever considered going back to that…that *creature!*'

Molly's estimation of Liam went up a thousand-fold. Which meant it was now off the planet. 'She is…was…very beautiful,' she said. 'And I dare say she was good in bed.'

Liam grimaced. 'I doubt anything about her is good except her acting. I would rather have five minutes in bed with you, Moll, than a lifetime with her. You leave her for dead in every department. And you're just as beautiful.'

Molly's heart caught. 'Not really, Liam,' she murmured. 'But it's nice of you to say so.'

'No, I mean it. You have a beauty which will last, because it comes from within. Not that I don't think you're very attractive,' he said as he drew her into his arms. 'You are. And very sexy too. In fact you're more sexy with your clothes on than Roxy is stark naked. I see now that true sexiness comes from what a woman subtly offers a man. A willingness to give as well as receive. And trust. It wasn't so much your virginity I found enchanting last night, but your trust. You trusted me with your body, and even your life. That blew me away. *You* blew me away. I couldn't sleep all night for thinking of you, and wanting you again. What I said to you earlier, Moll... I didn't really mean that. I would never do anything to hurt you. I was simply off my head with wanting you. And I was in a flat panic that you were going to go off and find someone else.'

She cupped his handsome face and tried to still her racing heart. 'You mean you're not going to bow me to your will through fair means or foul? You're not going to try to turn me into some kind of sex slave?'

'God, no. I don't know what got into me.'

'Well, that's a real shame,' she said, smiling saucily into his very serious face. 'I was rather looking forward to it.'

His blue eyes jerked wide, then narrowed.

'I have an awful feeling you mean that.'

'I do...in a fashion.'

'What kind of fashion?'

'I certainly wouldn't want you to ever hurt me. But I *was* looking forward to all those experiences you promised. And I rather fancied the idea of your becoming my sexual tutor...'

She reached up to kiss him lightly on the lips.

'And my master...'

She kissed him again, not quite so lightly.

'And my own personal devil...'

Her third kiss left him breathing heavily.

'But most of all,' she whispered huskily, 'I was counting on you taking me to that mysterious level of surrender not even dreamt of in my darkest, most decadent fantasy.'

His expression had darkened during her provocative confession. She wasn't sure if she'd shocked him to the core this time or not. He was certainly pretty still. But then a slow smile pulled at his nicely shaped mouth, and a wicked gleam brightened his beautiful blue eyes.

'You do know what happens to little girls who play with fire, Moll, don't you?'

She gulped. Had she gone too far?

'Er...'

'Too late,' he snapped, and scooped her up into his arms. 'You can't throw down a challenge like that to a man like me, then try to back out.' He began to stride towards the bedroom.

'But I... I...'

He halted in the doorway. 'You what? Speak now, woman, or for ever hold your peace.'

Molly bit her bottom lip and Liam swept into the room. At least he'd called her a woman!

CHAPTER FIFTEEN

'MOLL?'

Molly was lying crossways on the bed with her head cradled in the small of Liam's back. Liam was stretched out on his stomach, face buried in the pillows. Till a moment ago, she'd thought he was asleep.

And well he might have been. He had to be utterly exhausted. She herself was bone-weary.

But what an afternoon it had been! She would never have believed she could come so many times in a few short hours. Or that a man and woman could make love in so many different ways and positions.

Liam had seemed to delight in witnessing her shock at each successive and seemingly outrageous suggestion, before seducing her to his will with an ease that made a mockery of her initial inhibited reaction. How quickly he'd routed those inhibitions, showing her pleasures undreamt of, once she'd put aside—or at least learnt to ignore—that squirming embarrassment which came whenever he looked upon her body in some new and increasingly intimate fashion.

He'd become her own personal devil all right, tempting her in ways she might have read and dreamt about, but which she would never have believed she would dare to do.

Her stomach fluttered at what he might be going to suggest now, just when she'd thought everything had come to a satisfying conclusion. Was there anything else? She doubted it.

'Yes?' she murmured warily, her own eyes staying shut.

'Lift your head for a second, will you?'

She did, and he rolled over onto his back. 'Right. You can put your head back down again.'

Her head now nestled into his stomach, Molly's own stomach contracted. The nearness of his slumbering penis brought back hot memories of the last time she'd encountered his flagging desire, less than thirty minutes before. Liam had carried her into the shower after one of their torrid matings and, after washing her all over, had given her the shower gel and the sponge and set her to returning the favour.

She'd been shy at first, as she always was when confronted by one of Liam's new suggestions. Her hands had initially been hesitant on him, but not for long.

How exciting it had been to bring him to life again in such a stunningly intimate way. There'd been a dizzying sense of power at the sight of him growing harder and larger by the second, his moans letting her know how much he was enjoying her ministrations. The decision to sink to her knees and do to him what he'd already done to her more than once had come without conscious thought. It had seemed perfectly natural, yet at the same time the most wildly exciting thing she'd ever done.

Liam, however, had not been as comfortable with her bold lovemaking. His thighs had alternately trembled and tensed as he'd struggled to control himself.

'Stop,' he'd rasped at last, stiffening and bracing himself back against the cool, wet tiles. 'You must stop.'

But she had not stopped. If he'd been her own personal devil before, she was his at that moment, her lips tempting him with the dark excitement of total surrender to *her* will this time.

And while the hot water beat down on them both and the bathroom filled with steam Liam had finally lost his battle of the flesh, and she'd had her wicked way with him.

'Moll?' he said again, snapping her out of her erotic reverie.

She shivered then glanced up at him. 'What?'

He was staring down at her with heavy-lidded eyes.

'Why is it, do you think, that everyone seems to believe you're in love with me?'

Molly froze, then forced a light laugh. 'I didn't know everyone did. Surely you're not talking about Roxy? She was so green-eyed she couldn't see straight!'

'I realise that. But Dennis seemed to think so too. Then this morning even Mum hinted the same.'

Molly gulped. 'Really?'

'Yes, she said how much you cared for me and if

I hurt one hair on your head I'd have her to answer to.'

Molly was touched, but also flustered. Was this the moment to confess, to tell Liam the truth? How would he react, she wondered, to finding out *he* was the enigmatic and mysterious Mr X? Even if he was initially flattered, he might also be annoyed. He might think she'd made some kind of fool of him by playing with his own identity like that.

Liam would not like thinking that she'd been mocking him, or amusing herself at his expense. Which she *had* been, in a way. Though never maliciously.

Then there was his possible reaction to finding out she'd been pining for him all these years like a love-sick cow. Even Roxy had realised that if she declared a lifelong love and undying devotion Liam would have run a mile. His mother's advice had been similar. Liam was captivated by spirited women who went after what they wanted, not little mice who languished for years from an unrequited passion.

No, she could not tell him the truth. She could not risk losing Liam's respect, and possibly losing Liam. She might only have won his lust so far, but it was a start.

'Well, of course I *do* care for you, Liam,' she confessed rather nonchalantly. 'I always have.'

'Yes, but it's this Mr X you're in love with,' he muttered, none too happily. His disgruntlement gave Molly hope. He lifted his head to glare down at her. 'You *are* still in love with him, aren't you?'

She didn't know what to say. She really had to get rid of that infernal Mr X once and for all. He'd become a nuisance and an embarrassment.

But how?

'Well?' Liam glowered at her.

Incredibly, she blushed.

Liam took that for an admission, and scowled. 'What in God's name has *he* got that *I* haven't got?'

Now Molly was rattled. 'Er...nothing, I guess.'

'Then there's no reason why you can't fall out of love with him and in love with *me*, is there?'

Molly's mouth dropped open. 'What...what are you saying?'

'What am I saying?' He bent down and scooped her up on top of him. 'I'm saying I'm mad about you, Moll. And I won't rest till you're just as mad about me.' He rolled her under him and kissed her with a breathtaking hunger, his hands cupping her face and keeping it solidly captive beneath his. 'I know I can make you want me sexually,' he muttered after he'd reduced her to a panting mess. 'But that's not enough. I want to drive all thoughts of Mr X from your mind. I want you to love me as you've loved no other man.'

'But I already have, Liam. Loved you as I've loved no other man.'

His head jerked back. 'What?'

'Do you think I've done any of the things I've done with you today with any other man?'

He frowned. 'But I thought...I mean... Look, lots of girls out there are technically virgins these days, but that doesn't mean they haven't done plenty. I thought…in the shower…I mean… My God, Moll,' he said, awe in his voice, 'you're damned good at that for a beginner.'

'Perhaps I just have a damned good tutor,' she murmured, smiling. 'And perhaps you were right about Mr X. What I felt for him was probably only infatuation, a fantasy. To be honest, I haven't given him a thought all the time I've been with you.'

'So, you're not in love with him any more?'

'I can't see how I can be.'

His triumphant smile sent shivers down her spine. 'In that case *that's* going to be my next project— making you fall in love with me.'

Molly tried not to stare too hard. Or to cry.

But it was just too good to be true.

She swallowed and tried not to let her feelings overwhelm her. Common sense dictated she be careful and not get her hopes up too high. Liam might be mad about her at the moment but that didn't mean he genuinely loved her. It might all be one of his passing passions, a temporary obsession. He'd probably been mad about Roxy at one point, plus all those other girls.

'And how do you aim to do that?' she asked him with a saucy smile.

He pursed his lips and made a thoughtful sound. 'I'm not quite sure yet. You're much more of a mystery than I ever imagined. A highly complex girl, not the simple creature I thought I knew so well. And you're far naughtier than I'd imagined, too,' he added, his eyes gleaming.

'Really?' She laughed. 'Well, you're *exactly* as I always imagined.'

'Is that good or bad?'

'Oh, definitely good. *And* bad. You are as selfish as you said you were, but not in bed, thankfully.'

'I'm not going to be selfish any more,' he vowed. 'I'm going to change.'

She smiled. 'And the sun's going to rise in the west.'

'You just wait and see. Besides, who are you to talk? Moved-on-Made-over Molly isn't exactly all Miss Sweetness and Light. You could have knocked me over with a feather the way you stood up to Roxy out there.'

'Whereas the Molly I used to be would have stood there and not made a sound, not even a little squeak.'

'Hey. Don't run her down. I really liked that girl. She was sweet.'

Molly's eyebrows lifted. Yes, but you didn't fall in love with her, came the rueful thought.

'She was a bore!'

'She was *very* nice,' he defended hotly.

'She's dead and gone. Banished!'

'No, she's not,' he said, his voice dropping to a soft and sentimental timbre. 'She's still there, hiding underneath your new red hair and your newly found assertiveness. I think that's why my feelings for you are different to what they were with any of those other girls. Different, and deeper. Because *you're* different. I've always liked you, Moll. You're not a vain little puss. And you're honest as the day is long. You'd never lie to me, or try to manipulate me. You're the sort of girl a man is proud to take home to his mother. The sort of girl a man wants to m—'

She pushed her fingers against his mouth, panic flowering all through her. 'Hush! Don't say that, Liam. Don't!'

He groaned, then picked up her fingers and kissed the trembling fingertips. 'I'm rushing you, I know. I can be like that once I set my sights on something. I can see it's the wrong thing for me to do. Only yesterday you were a virgin, and in love with another man. I can understand you might be a little confused. But I can also be patient too,' he vowed passionately. 'And very single-minded. You're going to be mine, Moll. Fight me if you will. I enjoy a good fight. But come the new year you will be my fiancée, with my ring on your finger and true love for me in your heart.'

She stared at him with wide, blinking eyes. She almost told him then, but didn't. For she knew she had to make sure of him, had to let him fight his good fight for her, and for her love. It was fitting, after all the years of heartache and longing she'd been through, that he should not win her too easily.

Men did not value what they gained easily. And Liam was going to value her. She deserved it.

'The new year?' she said, her mind racing. That was ten months away, ten months of him chasing her, courting her, pursuing and seducing her. It was an irresistibly exciting thought. 'Well, I suppose by then I should know if it's a true love I feel for you and not just infatuation. After my fiasco with Mr X, I would want to be sure...'

'You'll be sure, my darling. Don't worry. I'll make sure of that!'

CHAPTER SIXTEEN

THE party was in full swing, a large and motley collection of people having gathered in the Delaney house to celebrate New Year's Eve, plus the engagement of Liam to his long-time girlfriend and next-door neighbour, Molly McCrae.

As the glamorous guests of honour, the happy couple were dressed for the part. The proud groom-to-be was resplendent in stylish navy trousers, an open-necked blue shirt and a suave cream silk sports jacket. His bride-to-be was stunning in a strapless party dress of emerald satin, with an even more stunning emerald and gold choker gracing her long, elegant neck. It had been a Christmas present from her adoring fiancé, one of many he'd lavished on her during the past year.

Liam had, in fact, spoiled Molly rotten with gifts of expensive clothes and jewellery, not to mention his myriad smaller purchases of chocolates, flowers and perfume. He'd taught her to drive in his precious new Mazda, and would have bought her a car, if she'd let him. Then there were the fantasy getaways he'd taken her on, weekends here and there at romantic places designed to seduce and soften even the hardest of hearts.

Not that Molly was a hard girl. Liam knew she wasn't.

But she'd been surprisingly difficult to win, he'd found to his consternation. He'd never been quite sure of her feelings. She'd kept him dangling, had often been late for dates, and had sometimes even dared to cancel them. He'd never quite known where he stood with her, which had been both irritating and intriguing.

Only in the lovemaking department had he been sure of his domination over her. There, she was putty in his hands, melting at his touch, quick to be aroused and always willing, no matter how often he wanted her, or where.

She'd never said no, even when there'd been some danger of being discovered. His choosing precarious places—such as behind rocks at the beach or in a sparsely filled movie theatre—had sometimes soothed the sense of emotional insecurity she instilled in him. At those moments when she'd been prepared to take any risk to have him, he'd almost felt loved. There'd been no doubt she craved him sexually; could not deny him. But was that love?

She'd never said she loved him. Not in so many words.

Till Christmas Day, when he'd produced an engagement ring for her which would have done Elizabeth Taylor proud. It was a huge brilliant-cut yellow Argyle diamond, set in gold. But it had been his words as he'd given it to her that had seemed to do the trick.

'This cost me a fortune, Moll,' he'd said. 'But a fortune means nothing to me without you. Marry me, my darling. I love you so much, and I think you love me. You don't have to say you do if you don't want to but it would be nice, just once, to hear it from your lips.'

Molly had stared at him and then burst into tears. He'd gathered her to him and heard the words he'd been dying to hear all year. 'Of course I love you. Don't you know that yet? I love you, Liam. Love you... Love you...'

He looked over at her now across the crowded living room and caught her eye. She smiled at him, green eyes sparkling. It wasn't so much different from smiles she'd given him before, but tonight he saw the love in them. Why hadn't he seen it before?

Liam was about to walk across the room to join her when someone tapped him on the elbow. 'Hello, you gorgeous hunk, you. If I wasn't married, you know, I'd have given Molly a run for her money.'

It was Joan, from the library, Molly's friend.

Liam smiled. 'You would have had to be good.'

Joan nodded up and down. 'You're right. Molly's a grand girl and I'm very happy for her. You don't know how lucky you are.'

'Oh, I think I do...'

'She's loved you for so long, you know.'

Liam was about to say he didn't know at all when

he stopped himself. It was then he realised Joan was off in another world, smiling at something in her head.

'I can still remember the day she came into the library and told me about Mr X. You must remember Mr X, Liam,' she added, glancing up at him.

'Only too well,' Liam said drily, and lifted the glass he was holding to his lips.

Joan chuckled. 'I nearly cracked up when she told me about him, especially when she said you hadn't twigged. I mean…you have to admit it's very funny, but rather typical of men, not seeing beyond their nose. But I dare say you've laughed together about it since.'

'Laughed about what?'

'About your being Mr X, of course.'

Liam's drink froze midway to his mouth. He stared at Joan over the glass. She grimaced, then groaned. 'Oh, dear heaven, you didn't know. I always assumed she'd told you. Oh, Lord!'

Liam could hardly think. *He* was Mr X. His head spun with the news, and all it implied. Molly had loved him all along. But she'd also lied to him, laughed at him, manipulated him. She'd been a schemer, as Roxy had warned she was.

He recoiled at this thought, and his feelings showed on his face.

'Don't you *dare* take that attitude,' Joan warned. 'Don't you *dare!* That girl loves you. No, she adores you. Always has done. But did you ever see it? Not on your nelly! You sailed on through your glamorous, privileged life, tossing her a few crumbs from your table when it suited you. You didn't give a fig for her feelings. You took her for granted and you broke her heart.'

'But that's not—'

'Oh, do shut up and listen!' Joan snapped. 'So what if she protected her self-esteem by inventing a Mr X? So what if she had some fun with it? She'd had little enough fun in her life at that point in time. Give credit where credit is due, Liam. When she saw her chance, she went after what she wanted. She changed for you, lied for you, fought for you. And she won you, by God—won your love and your respect. Look at her, Liam. She's a beautiful and very brave woman; a woman in a million. Don't you dare tell her I told you about Mr X. Don't take away her pride. Go on letting her think you believe she once had a Mr X in her life, because maybe she needs that. Maybe she… Oh, my God, she's coming over. Promise me, Liam. Promise me you won't tell her I told you.'

'I promise, Joan,' he said faithfully. 'And thank you…for making me finally see the light.'

Liam watched the girl he loved walk towards them, a lovely smile on her lovely face. He felt humbled and incredibly moved as the full import of Joan's words sank in. Molly had always loved him. Oh, how cruel life could be sometimes. And how wonderful.

He saw now why he loved her so much. Because she loved *him* so much. He must have sensed it at some subconscious level, had known that to let her go would be the worst, most stupid thing he could ever do. He vowed now he would never let her go. Never!

'What are you two sneaky devils talking about over here?' she asked, glancing from one to the other. 'You were looking very serious, Joan. You too, darling.'

Liam's heart kicked over. Never had the word 'darling' on her lips sounded so sweet, or so touching. He wound his arm around her slender waist and pulled her against him.

'We were having a very serious discussion on having children in this day and age, weren't we, Joan? We agreed it's a difficult task being a parent, but I'm willing to risk it anyway.'

He could see the flicker of surprised pleasure in her eyes. 'I've been wanting to discuss children with you. I...I would like to have a baby quite soon, but I wasn't sure about you...'

No, he thought, understanding dawning. She still wasn't sure of him. It was a cruel legacy of all those years when he hadn't noticed her, hadn't wanted her. That was why she'd kept *him* unsure. She'd been protecting herself, had made him keep proving his love over and over. There was still a lot of work to be done, he realised, before she would feel totally secure in his love. But having children together would be a good start.

He gave her a reassuring smile, and a loving little squeeze. 'How soon is soon?'

She gave a self-conscious laugh. 'How about nine months after the wedding day?'

'How about six?' he returned, squeezing her again. The wedding date had been set in March.

'I think this conversation is getting too private for me,' Joan quipped, and was off.

Liam laughed. 'I like your Joan. I think we'll ask her to be godmother to our first child.'

'Our...*first* child?'

'You don't honestly think we're going to have only one child, do you? Only children are notoriously spoiled.'

'Yes, well...'

He kissed her. Then kissed her again. 'Do you think we might slip away somewhere?' he murmured against her trembling mouth.

'Where? We can't possibly be gone long and people have infiltrated your whole house, even your bedroom.'

'What about yours?'

Molly sucked in a startled breath. 'Mine? But it...it only has a single bed in it.'

Liam took her hand and began drawing her from the room. 'Single beds were just made for lovers.'

Midnight came with cheers and shouts, whistles and car horns. People spilled out of houses into the street below. Everyone was kissing.

No one missed the guests of honour.

Nine months later, a baby was born to Mr and Mrs

Liam Delaney. A boy. The grandmothers were delighted, and even approved of his name. Saxon. But their joy was nothing compared to the mother's. Having Liam's child in her arms finally put to rest that little niggle of doubt which till then had plagued Molly: that it wasn't *her* he really loved, but the myth she'd created, that made-over moved-on version who was partly a pretend person.

But she'd known, during the long, painful hours of labour, when she'd hardly been looking her best, when she'd been crying and swearing and sweating, that the man holding her hand and mopping her brow really loved *her*, Molly, the person. She'd seen it in his concern, his patience, his tenderness. But mostly she'd seen it in his eyes, his beautiful blue eyes, the windows to his soul.

And that soul was full of true love for her.

Liam loved her, Molly, the simple, solid girl who'd always loved him.

She would never doubt it again, and he would never give her cause to.

Passion

Looking for stories that *sizzle?*
Wanting a read that has a little extra *spice?*

Every other month throughout 1999,
Harlequin Presents® is thrilled to bring you
romances that turn up the heat!

Look out for:

The Seduction Project by Miranda Lee
Harlequin Presents #2003, January 1999

The Marriage Surrender by Michelle Reid
Harlequin Presents #2014, March 1999

Marriage Under Suspicion by Sara Craven
Harlequin Presents #2026, May 1999

*Pick up a **PRESENTS PASSION**—
where **seduction** is guaranteed!*

Available wherever Harlequin books are sold.

HARLEQUIN®
Makes any time special ™

Coming Next Month

HARLEQUIN PRESENTS®

THE BEST HAS JUST GOTTEN BETTER!

**#2007 THE VENGEFUL HUSBAND Lynne Graham
(The Husband Hunters)**
To claim her inheritance and save her home, Darcy needed a husband, *fast!* Her advertisement was answered by Gianluca Raffacani—and while *he* wasn't aware he was her child's father, *she* didn't know he wanted revenge....

**#2008 THE SEXIEST MAN ALIVE Sandra Marton
(Valentine)**
Finding the Sexiest Man Alive to feature in *Chic* magazine was Susannah's last hope to stop Matt Romano from taking it over. But Matt insisted on assisting her and seducing her. Was he the world's sexiest man...?

#2009 IN BED WITH THE BOSS Susan Napier
Duncan had never forgotten his one night of passion with his secretary, Kalera, even if she had. Now she was engaged to another man...and Duncan vowed to entice her back to *his* bed...for good!

**#2010 EXPECTANT MISTRESS Sara Wood
(Expecting!)**
Four years after their first brief affair, Adam and Trish were back together again, and she was wondering if this was another fling.... But before she could tell him she was pregnant with his baby, she received a fax from his fiancée....

**#2011 ONE BRIDEGROOM REQUIRED! Sharon Kendrick
(Wanted: One Wedding Dress)**
Holly had the dress; now she needed a groom! Then she met Luke who was perfect—except that he wanted an *un*consummated marriage! If Holly was to have the perfect wedding *night*, this virgin would have to seduce her husband!

**#2012 A FORBIDDEN DESIRE Robyn Donald
(50th Book)**
Paul McAlpine found Jacinta mesmerizing, and now they would be spending the whole summer together. But he had to resist her—after all, she was engaged to another man....